Room for
just a little bit
More

BETH EHEMANN

CRANBERRY INN SERIES, VOLUME III

ALSO BY BETH EHEMANN

Room for You

Room for More

Room for *just a little bit* More

BETH EHEMANN

CRANBERRY INN SERIES, VOLUME III

Montlake
Romance

Text copyright © 2014 Beth Ehemann
All rights reserved.

Published by Montlake Romance, Seattle

www.apub.com

Amazon, the Amazon logo, and Montlake Romance are trademarks of Amazon.com, Inc., or its affiliates.

ISBN-13: 9781477829585
ISBN-10: 147782958X

Cover design by Shasti O'Leary-Soudant / SOS CREATIVE LLC

Library of Congress Control Number: 2014958171

Printed in the United States of America

To my husband, Chris, who taught me what unconditional love is. You often say that you're lucky to be with me, but I'm really the lucky one. Thank you for all the swoony inspiration you've provided over the last seventeen years. You'll always be my Brody.

1

KACIE

"Hello? Earth to Kacie! Are you gonna stare at that thing all day or what?"

My eyes shifted from my engagement ring to Alexa, who was sitting across the island from me. "You've had one of these for a million years now. I've had mine less than a day. Cut me some slack."

She rolled her eyes and leaned back, stretching her lower back. "Yeah, yeah. In a week, it'll be old news. Trust me."

"What's your problem, Negative Nancy?"

"This kid is the problem. It's what, the size of an apple right now? How can it be causing me pain already?" She grimaced.

"Everything is stretching and moving. It's probably gonna hurt for a while, unfortunately."

"Yeah, well, remind me to ground him when he comes out."

I laughed. "Today it's a he? Yesterday it was she."

"Who the hell knows what it is?" She threw her arms up in frustration. "Derek wants it to be a surprise and it's driving me crazy. He wants that delivery-room moment to be magical, and all I'm worried about is my vagina stretching out and all of my organs sliding across the floor."

I chuckled. "That's slightly dramatic, don't you think?"

"Hell no!" Her eyebrows pulled together as she glared at me. "I've watched *Grey's Anatomy*. I've watched those women scream and beat the crap out of their husbands."

"It's fake, Lex. All for TV, I promise. If you ever change your mind about finding out, I just might know someone with access to an ultrasound machine." I winked.

"I'll have to remember that the next time he refuses to go get me cream cheese wontons at one o'clock in the morning. Telling him the sex of his child would be the perfect payback."

"If you say so." I turned to the fridge and grabbed a bowl of grapes, setting them between us.

"So, enough about the devil child. Let's plan this wedding." She wiggled her eyebrows.

"I just got engaged last night!"

"Yeah, and if you want to have your reception at Graybil Gardens or Beelow Hall, you better book today. Those are the best places to get married within a fifty-mile radius, Kacie." She reached over and grabbed a few grapes, popping them into her mouth. "I had a woman come in last year to finalize her flower order who told me that she'd booked Graybil Gardens three years earlier and didn't even *meet* her fiancé until a year later."

My mouth fell open. "Seriously?"

"Yep." She nodded slowly. "Talk about being optimistic, huh?"

"Or desperate," I joked.

"Obviously," she agreed, "but my point is all those places book up fast. You might even have to ask Brody to use his star power to get you in."

Brody and I had been engaged roughly fifteen hours. I was on such a euphoric high from him asking me to marry him, I hadn't even thought about the actual wedding itself, nor was I in any hurry to, but Alexa was stressing me out.

"Lex, we haven't discussed any of that. We haven't picked a date, talked about a location. We haven't even told Lucy and Piper yet."

"What the hell are you guys waiting for?"

I shrugged. "I don't know. We wanted to tell them together, and Brody told Fred he'd help him organize a bunch of stuff in the garage today."

"You two are the weirdest people I know," she accused playfully.

"Why?"

"Maybe not both of you, but you for sure."

"Me?"

"Yes, you."

"Why?" I shrieked.

"Most women have been planning their weddings since they were five. You're the exception. I doubt you've ever really thought about your dream wedding." She stared right at me, waiting for an answer.

I looked down at the island and tried hard to remember a time I'd given serious thought to my wedding, but I couldn't find one. "You're right." My gaze lifted back to hers. "At one point in time, *years ago*, I had hoped to marry Zach, but I always figured with our money situation it would be a courthouse thing. Once we split, I never really thought about it again."

"Well, I definitely don't think the money thing is going to be an issue now." She chuckled.

"No, but some big, fancy wedding isn't really my thing either." I cringed at the thought of anything too stuffy. "You know that."

"Better than anyone." She grinned, shaking her head. "What time is it?"

I looked down at my phone. "Ten fifteen."

Her eyes bulged. "Crap! Gotta go. I have a doctor's appointment."

We slid off our stools and I followed her to the front door.

"Good news, though." She turned to me once she got to the foyer. "You won't have to worry about the flowers."

A sigh of relief left my mouth in a hurry. "Thank God. I was worried about that."

"You were?"

"Yeah. You'll have the baby by then. I didn't know if you'd want to do it or—"

"Shut up," she interrupted. "Of course I'd still do your wedding flowers for you. This baby isn't going to change our day-to-day life, Kacie."

"Oh, really?"

"Yes, really."

"Okay. We'll see if you still say that once he's here," I replied confidently.

She narrowed her eyes at me but kept quiet.

"Or she." I tried to stifle my laugh.

Alexa shot me a quick glare and disappeared out the door.

An hour later, the girls were playing out back with my mom and I was in and out of sleep on the couch in the living room when Brody sat down next to me, gently gliding his lips along my neck. His hot breath made all of my little hairs stand up. I cracked a smile as a small moan escaped my lips, but my eyes were too heavy to open.

"Wake up, Sleepyhead."

Still smiling, I shook my head.

"No?" He laughed.

"Shhh. I'm sleeping."

He gave my shoulders a small shake. "The girls are heading up the hill with your mom. Let's tell 'em!"

I cracked one eye open and peeked at him. The fact that he was as excited as I was about our engagement was beyond adorable, but wait . . .

Sitting up quickly, I squinted at the bright sun coming through the French doors. "How are we gonna tell them? Are we just going to blurt it out? We haven't talked about it."

"Kacie, not everything has to be planned out." He grinned as he tucked a piece of my wild hair behind my ear. "Let's just see what happens."

Before I could argue, the doors flew open and Lucy and Piper came into the room, arguing over whether the frog they'd just seen by the lake had yellow or blue eyes.

"Morning, Twinkies!" Brody smiled at them.

"Brody!" Lucy ran and jumped into his arms. Her tiny hands cupped his cheeks and she frowned at him. "Where were you this morning? We didn't see you."

He leaned forward and kissed the tip of her nose. "I was waaaaaay in the back of the garage helping Fred organize a bunch of boxes and stuff."

Piper's eyes grew huge as she took a step forward. "Did you see a spider?"

"I did." He laughed. "A few of them, actually."

Piper shuddered. "I hate spiders."

I reached out and wrapped my arms around her waist, pulling her in close so I could nuzzle my nose into her hair. She smelled like sunscreen and fresh grass. "I know you do, baby. But don't worry. They're way, way in the back of the garage."

"I hate spiders too." Brody smiled sweetly at her as he grazed her cheek with the backs of his fingers. "But I promise to always kill all the spiders for you."

Piper didn't say anything, simply offering a shy smile in return.

"Hey, I have a question for you guys. What's your absolute favorite Disney movie?" Brody looked back and forth between the two of them.

They looked at each other for a split second before blurting out, "*Cinderella!*"

"Mine too!" He looked at me and winked before returning his gaze to them. "You know how after the prince tried the slipper on Cinderella and it fit, they got married and lived happily ever after?"

The girls nodded, their eyes fixed on Brody's face as they hung on every word he was saying.

"Well, last night I asked your mom to marry me." His hand slid over and covered mine, squeezing it gently. "And guess what? She said yes!"

A tiny gasp sprang from Lucy, and Piper's mouth dropped open, both of them looking stunned. Their big brown eyes looked back and forth between Brody and me until Lucy turned and threw her arms around Piper's shoulders. They started hugging and jumping up and down excitedly.

I frowned and looked curiously at Brody. While I was happy they were so excited, their reaction was unexpected.

Then I learned *why* they were so thrilled.

"We get to live in a castle! We get to live in a castle!" they sang out as they jumped in circles, pumping their little arms up and down.

"Wait, wait, wait." I held my hands up, trying to get their attention. "Do they think—"

"Yes," I interrupted Brody, quickly turning back to the girls. "Guys, guys, listen."

They stopped jumping, but their smiles still clung to their faces.

I sighed, not wanting to crush their sweet little dreams, but unless Brody was the prince of some faraway country in Europe and forgot to tell me, we were most likely not gonna live in a castle.

"Ugh, I don't know how to break it to you guys, but we aren't gonna live in a castle," I said quietly.

Their faces fell like someone had just given them a puppy and then quickly taken it away, or in this case a castle.

"But . . . in *Cinderella* they live in a castle," Lucy whined.

"I know they do, baby, but we don't have a castle," I explained.

"Where are we gonna live, then?" Piper asked.

Crap.

"Well . . . um . . ." I looked at Brody, desperately searching his face for an answer. "We'll probably live—"

"We'll get a castle," Brody blurted out, a huge grin spread across his face.

"Yay!" they cheered and started dancing again.

"Wait." I reached out and tried to stop them, but they'd moved too far out into the room. They spun round and round as I turned toward Brody, staring blankly at him. "You know they're six and they remember *everything*, right?"

"I know," he confirmed proudly, his mischievous green eyes smiling at me.

"Brody, you just promised them a castle. Like . . . a castle!" I repeated incredulously, thinking he must not have heard me the first time.

"I know." He laughed as he watched the girls celebrate. "But look at them. How could I not? Don't worry. I'll figure something out." He reached over and patted my thigh.

Oddly enough, I believed him.

2

BRODY

"What the fuck is this, man?" Viper bellowed as he walked into Scooter Joe's Café and dropped the newspaper on my table.

"Good morning to you too." I laughed, picking it up.

Front page. Top story. Bold letters.

SORRY, LADIES! MINNESOTA'S MOST ELIGIBLE BACHELOR IS OFF THE MARKET:
Brody Murphy Proposes to Girlfriend Kacie Jensen

"What the hell? How do they know already?" I growled in frustration as I slammed the paper facedown on the table. As annoyed as I was with the headline, I was even more annoyed with the picture they added below it of Kacie and me at the zoo with the girls. Lucy and Piper were facing the other way, so thankfully no one could see their faces, but it still pissed me off. Kacie and I had talked long ago about my life and how it's in the spotlight more than I'd like, and she swore to me that we were worth it and she could handle it, but when they started posting pictures of her daughters, all bets were off.

Viper pulled the chair out and plopped down across from me. "The question is, how do *they* know before *me*?"

I smiled at him and shrugged. "Sorry. It just happened a couple days ago. I wanted to tell you in person. That's why I asked you to meet me for breakfast."

"Well, congratulations." He reached across and shook my hand.

"Thanks."

"You sure you're ready for this?"

"I'm more than ready." I sat up, looking him straight in the eye. "I want to marry that girl today, before she realizes she can do way better than me and changes her mind."

Viper sat still for a minute, not responding. Just before I opened my mouth to talk, he batted his eyes at me and clapped his hands together. "Awww. There's no one better than you, Brody Murphy," he joked in an annoyingly high-pitched voice.

"Cut the shit, Finkle." I laughed. "You're just jealous I didn't save myself for you."

"True," he agreed, "but we could always have some scorching affair and really give the magazines something to talk about. Do you like being on top or bottom?"

I held my hand over my mouth, concentrating desperately on not spitting my coffee out. "Okay, that was a little much."

Viper laughed heartily and smacked his hand down on the table loudly, causing a couple of people to turn and look at us. "All jokes aside, I'm happy for you, man. I really am. She's a great girl, but you're right . . . definitely out of your league."

I looked down at the table and thought about Kacie and how I couldn't wait to spend the rest of my life with her. Lucy and Piper, the kids we would eventually make together, holidays, graduations, vacations . . . those were all the big things I was looking forward to, but with her I wanted more. I wanted all the awesome little things too.

Sleeping in on Sundays, date nights at my favorite little Italian place in the city, all of our weird inside jokes, her cinnamon rolls. I wanted all of it, every single day.

"Jesus, wipe the goofy smile off your face." Viper threw a wadded-up napkin at me, laughing when it bounced off my forehead.

"Sorry." I shook my head back to reality. "Hey, I actually asked you here for another reason, not just because I wanted to see your ugly face."

"Oh, this should be interesting." He sat back in his chair and locked his fingers behind his head.

"Unfortunately, there aren't a lot of guys on the team I can stomach and my choices are limited," I joked, "so I wanted to know if you would stand up with me in our wedding?"

"Seriously?" he asked excitedly, sitting up straight.

I laughed. "Yes. Seriously."

He clapped his hands together and rubbed them as an evil smile spread across his face. "I'm so ready. Do I get to be best man?"

"Unfortunately, no. That job is reserved for Andy. Sorry." I shrugged.

"Really?" he whined. "Fine, but I get to plan the bachelor party."

"Oh, Jesus," I sighed, dropping my head into my hands.

Viper laughed wickedly and took his phone out.

"What are you doing?" I asked.

Frowning in concentration down at his phone, he moved his fingers back and forth as fast as he could. "Midget strippers. Jell-O wrestling. Camel rides. Booking it all now." He looked up at me quickly. "You're not allergic to maple syrup, are you?"

"Oh my God, put the damn phone down." I rolled my eyes, reaching over and grabbing it from him. I set it on the table in between us. "Let's not talk about anything wedding—or bachelor party—related for ten minutes, okay?"

"Fine." He pouted like a child who'd just been scolded.

"So, I haven't talked to you in a few days. What's new with you? Seen Darla lately?"

"Actually, yes. We went to a movie Monday night."

My mouth fell open. I couldn't believe what I was hearing. "Wait. You took her on a date? Like an out-of-the-bedroom date?"

"Yep. I mean, I tried to get her to suck my dick in the theater, but she had a fit. I had no choice but to watch the whole fucking movie." He sighed.

"Oh, you poor, sex-deprived maniac," I condescended.

"How you guys doing? You okay?" Joe asked as he walked up to our table. "Need anything?"

"I think we're still good. Thanks, Joe." I smiled and nodded at him.

"Joe, did you know this idiot is getting married?" Viper pointed across the table in my direction.

"I did hear something about that this morning." Joe looked from Viper to me, a smile spreading across his face. "Two hot little blonds were talking about it when I was getting their drinks. I asked who they were talking about and they showed me the paper."

"This one?" Viper picked it up and showed it to him.

"Yeah, that was it." He nodded, taking the paper from Viper and examining it closely. "I gotta say, you picked a good one, Brody. Nice little ass on her." Joe slapped my shoulder in congratulations before he walked away.

I watched Joe walk across the coffee shop until he was behind the counter, out of earshot, and I looked back at Viper. "There's something wrong with him, you know that?"

Viper laughed and slammed his hand down again so hard it made our cups rattle against the table. "Are you kidding? I love him. He's a horny old man, my hero. I want to be Joe when I grow up."

"Be serious. You're never growing up." I threw the balled-up napkin back at him.

"You're right," he agreed. "No way will you ever catch me putting a diamond on some chick's finger and getting down on one knee. Fuck that."

"Come on." I tilted my head to the side. "Never?"

"Nope. Never. My parents have been married and divorced enough times for me to learn that marriage just doesn't work."

He was shaking his head back and forth defiantly, but I knew even *he* didn't believe the bullshit he was spewing. Somewhere deep inside that walking hard-on was a man who needed a serious girl to straighten his ass out. I just wasn't in the mood to argue with him.

After I pretended to listen as Viper went on and on about conventional marriage and how pointless it was for another hour, I headed to Andy's office. When I was there a few days ago signing my contract, I'd told him I was going to propose, but I hadn't talked to him since.

The elevator doors opened and I was greeted with Ellie's cheery smile.

"Hey, Brody." She sat back from her computer. "Congratulations!"

"Thanks," I said proudly. "I'm assuming you guys saw the paper too?"

"Uh, yeah. It's been the chatter around the office this morning. Actually"—she looked off into space, frowning slightly—"it's kinda been the buzz all over. I was getting my gas this morning and even the people on the other side of the pump were talking about it."

"Wow. Gas station gossip. Guess that means I've arrived, huh?" I laughed as I shoved my hands in my pockets and walked toward Andy's office.

"Wait a sec, don't go in yet. He has a client in there, but I think they're just about done."

"Okay, no problem." I sat on the couch. The morning's newspaper sat on top of the stack of magazines on the coffee table, taunting me. I shoved it to the side and started sifting through the magazines when Andy's office door opened.

A young woman who looked to be in her early twenties, probably not even bar legal, walked out with her ponytail swinging behind her. I stood up and took a step toward Andy's office just as he appeared in the doorway, leaning against the frame. Hiding myself behind a tall plant, I watched him watch *her* walk away. She got to the elevator, pushed the button, and turned back to him, a shy smile creeping across her face.

"Bye, Andy," she cooed.

Ellie's head snapped up from whatever she was working on, and she stared at the girl. The ding of the elevator broke their *Lady and the Tramp* stare at each other, and Andy offered a one-handed wave before she bounced in and disappeared.

Lady and the Tramp? I'm clearly watching too much Disney.

"Andy?" Ellie repeated sarcastically. "Don't your clients call you Mr. Shaw?"

Andy cleared his throat and looked at the ground as his face flushed. "Uh, yeah."

"Except for me, of course," I bragged, taking a step forward so he could see me.

Andy's eyes widened at my sudden appearance. "What the hell are *you* doing here?"

"I came to talk to you, though it looks like you'd like to talk to her some more." I nodded my head toward the elevator. "Want to chase her down? I can wait in your office."

Andy rolled his eyes. "Shut up and get in here."

I walked past him into his office, with him following along behind me. "Ellie, hold my calls for a bit, okay?" he called out before closing the door.

"So, who is that mystery woman? Wait. Is she even a woman? Mystery teenager?" I teased as I plopped down on his couch.

"Fuck you. She's a client." He sounded annoyed as he sat in the chair across from me.

"That doesn't answer my question." I laughed. "What's her name?"

"Callie Marsh. She's a tennis player."

"Hmmm. Limber," I cracked, ducking just in time from the football flying toward my head.

"I haven't dated her, nor am I going to date her. You know my rule about clients."

"I do, but I also saw the way you watched her leave." I picked up the football and tossed it back to him. "Rules are made to be broken, my friend."

"Ha!" he laughed out loud. "Says the all-American boy who just got engaged to the all-American girl who comes built-in with the most perfect all-American family ever. Congratulations, asswipe."

"Thank you. I think."

"Have you set a date yet?"

"Not even close." I got up and walked over to the bar area of his office and grabbed a water bottle out of his fridge. "Other than telling the girls yesterday, we've barely even talked about it. Want one?" I held up the bottle.

"Sure." I tossed the bottle to him. "Thanks. What do you mean you've barely talked about it?"

Walking back to the couch, I groaned. "You know, Alexa said the same thing to Kacie yesterday. Why is everyone thinking we should've had this planned already?"

"I don't know, but you weren't kidding when you said everyone. Once that newspaper hit the street this morning and the article went online, I got three e-mails from banquet hall owners offering their services." He cracked his water bottle open and took a swig.

"You did?"

"Yep. Apparently they think I'm your wedding planner, not your agent."

"Actually, funny you should mention that, I do need your help with something." I shifted uncomfortably on the couch. Andy had been my best friend as far back as I could remember, but I was nervous about asking him to be my best man. Viper was easy. I knew he'd be all over it. While I didn't necessarily think Andy would say no, I knew he had a lot of shit going on. Part of me felt like no matter what, he would always be the non-biological older brother I would constantly seek validation from.

"So, I know life is crazy for you right now, and I don't want to add to that"—I rubbed my sweaty palms on the thighs of my jeans—"but I would be honored if you would stand up next to me and be my best man."

Andy sat in his chair like the boss that he was, completely confident and relaxed as he rubbed his top lip with his thumb and stared back at me, making me wait longer than I was comfortable with for his response.

"Brody, you're right. My life is crazy. The phones are ringing off the hook since you signed that huge-ass contract the other day. Blaire is as obnoxious as ever, dragging me in and out of court for money every ten minutes, and being a single dad is way harder than anything I do inside this office."

Oh, shit. I'm going to have to beg Viper, aren't I?

"But . . . that all being said, do you honestly think for one minute I'd pass up standing shoulder to shoulder with my best friend when he gets married?" He stood up and offered his hand to me. "And *I'm* the one who's honored, friend."

3

KACIE

It was late when Brody got back to my house. He'd gone to the city for the day to talk to Viper and Andy, and though I told him he didn't have to come back for the night since it was going to be so late, he insisted, and I didn't argue.

Mom, Fred, and I were sitting on the couch when we heard the front door open. I hopped up and tried not to jog up front.

"Hey," I welcomed him, throwing my arms around his neck. His big arms wrapped around me, squeezing so hard it made my chest ache, but I didn't dare tell him for fear that he'd quit hugging me like that every time.

"Hey, babe. How was your day?" He loosened the hug but didn't let go.

"Good. How was yours? How did everything go?"

I squirmed out of his arms and we walked hand in hand to the living room.

"Hi, Brody!" Mom called out when we got to the kitchen, Fred offering a silent wave.

"Hey, guys," Brody responded, sounding exhausted.

"You okay?" I gently rubbed the side of his face as he sat down at the island. "Can I get you something?"

"No, thanks. I'm good, just tired. It was a long day." He smiled. "But everything went well. Viper said he'd be in the wedding, then proceeded to book every illegal activity in Minnesota for a bachelor party."

"Oh boy." I laughed nervously, setting a glass of ice water in front of him.

"Thanks, and don't worry. I told him to chill out. I will definitely have a say in what we do." He paused and took a long drink of the water he'd said he didn't need. "Then I went to Andy's. We ended up talking longer than I'd planned on, and he asked me to go have a burger and a beer with him, so I did."

"I'm glad you had such a good day."

"All right, you crazy kids." Mom walked over to us with Fred following right behind. "Us old folks are heading to bed. Turn the lights off when you're done?"

"Got it, Mom." I yawned, suddenly feeling just as tired as Brody looked.

She leaned over and kissed my forehead before she and Fred disappeared down the hall.

Brody rested his chin on his fist and smiled lazily at me, his beautiful green eyes sparkling. "You look tired too."

"I wasn't until you got home." I yawned again. "Suddenly I'm ready for bed."

Brody cocked an eyebrow at me as the corner of his mouth pulled up in a sexy smirk. "Ready for bed, or ready for Brody?"

"Well, I meant bed, but I could possibly be persuaded into something else." I giggled.

"No, if you're really tired, we'll just go to bed."

"I'm tired. I'm stressed. I'm just . . . blah."

"Wanna talk about it?" He reached over and squeezed my hand.

I shrugged halfheartedly.

"Come on." Pulling me to a stand, he held on to my hand and led me to the living room, where we both sat on the couch. He lifted my feet into his lap and started massaging them as he looked at me. "What's going on? Talk to me."

"I think Alexa's comments yesterday are bothering me more than I initially thought."

"How so?"

"I don't know. I just feel like a slacker because we haven't picked the wedding date and location and a dress and everything else, all within forty-eight hours of being engaged." I sighed.

"Ah." He nodded. "*Those* comments. Yeah, I kinda got the same thing from Andy today."

"You did?"

Who knew guys talked about wedding planning too?

"Yeah, he actually said he got a few e-mails this morning from different places offering to host our reception."

"Holy shit, seriously? I don't get it. Why do so many people care where we get married?"

Brody shrugged and shook his head as he continued the best foot massage ever given by any human ever. "Publicity, probably. Then they can forever say they held Brody and Kacie's wedding there."

I tilted my head to the side and narrowed my eyes at him skeptically. "Gimme a break. They don't care about the Kacie part. They just want to be able to say Brody Murphy got married there. Who you're marrying is irrelevant."

"Not to me," he said sweetly, trying to make me feel better.

"Oh, I know and it's okay. I couldn't care less what the public or whoever thinks of our wedding. It's for us, you and me, and that's all that matters."

"I'm glad you feel that way." He bent his leg under him and turned to face me. "I had a thought while I was driving home."

I rolled my eyes. "I'm not eloping."

"No, no. I know that. But you're right . . . about not letting *them* have our wedding, the paparazzi and leeches who thought it was okay to post a picture of the girls in the newspaper. I don't want them having any part in our day, so I was thinking, what if we had the ceremony and the reception in my parents' barn?"

My mouth fell open as he held his hand up. "Don't freak. Just hear me out. I know it's a crappy, run-down barn, but I was thinking how cool it might look if we hung thousands of little white lights or even candles everywhere, though we don't want to burn it down, but you get what I'm saying," he rambled, barely taking a breath. "I can hire a company to come in and clean it up. We'll rent some tables and chairs and whatever other crap you need for a wedding. Anything you want, Kacie. The sky's the limit. I just want you to be—"

I put my hand over his mouth to stop the adorable, incoherent sentences that were tumbling out of his mouth.

When he stopped talking against my hand, I lowered it and scooted forward, cupping his face in my hands. I looked him straight in the eye. "Brody, I think that's the best idea I have *ever* heard."

"Really?" His eyebrows shot up in surprise.

"Yes, really. I don't want our celebration at some stuffy banquet hall where two thousand other people have gotten married. I want ours to be special, and I can't think of a more special place than your parents' barn."

A devilish grin spread across his face. "We do have history in that barn, don't we?"

"Correction." I moved closer to him and gently brushed my nose against his. "We *almost* had history in that barn. The girls came in and interrupted us, remember?" I gently kissed the corner of his mouth and flicked his lips with my tongue.

"How could I forget? I still don't think my balls have recovered."

"Oh, please." I ran my teeth gently along his jawline and kissed just under his ear. "We've had sex like five hundred times since then."

His hand clutched my thigh and squeezed gently as he started breathing heavier. "If you keep kissing me like this and then go to sleep, I'm gonna have navy-blue balls all over again."

"I'm not tired anymore."

"You aren't?" Pleasant surprise filled his voice.

"Nope." I moved my tongue to the other side of his neck while my fingers ran up his thigh, under his shorts. "You said the magic word."

"What did I say? Wait. I said barn." His hearty laugh vibrated under my lips.

"You said barn," I reiterated. "And you know what that does to me."

"I do, but I didn't know it could take you from zero to a hundred that fast. I'll have to remember that for the next fifty years. Screw that, I'm getting it tattooed on me somewhere."

"Stop talking," I ordered, pulling away just enough to look him in the eye, "and kiss me."

The words were barely out of my mouth before Brody's strong hands encompassed my face, gently pulling my lips to his. The second we connected, all the tiny stresses of the last couple of days washed away. He held a secret power that I hadn't known existed until we got together. Contact with Brody actually altered the way I felt physically. If I was sick, he would hold my hand, and I'd feel better. If I was angry, he would hug me and make it all disappear. And in moments like this, when I was hot for him, his smallest touch set me on fire.

After four swipes of his tongue, I was straddling him on my couch, grinding my hips into him as hard as I could.

"Whoa," he laughed. "Slow down there, killer, or we're both gonna need Neosporin tomorrow."

"It'd be worth it." I continued kissing him.

"For you, it's worth a little chafing, but I'd rather be skin to skin, and I'm thinking the couch in the family room isn't the ideal location. Wanna move this down the hall?"

He was right.

Mom had a full house of guests, and I didn't think any of them wanted to see the innkeeper's daughter dry humping her fiancé on the common area sofa, even if that fiancé was a smokin'-hot hockey superstar.

Okay, maybe they would want to see it, then, but I wanted to keep our life together as private as possible. I could just imagine Brody getting a call from Andy in the morning freaking out that some weirdo had videoed us on the couch and our sex tape was all over the Internet. Kim Kardashian could keep that disgusting throne; I had no interest in it.

"Yes, let's go," I whispered, sliding off of him.

I grabbed his hand and pulled him along behind me, down the hall.

"Wait. Do you want to go to your room or mine?" He stopped suddenly, tugging my hand back. "We don't want the girls to hear us."

"Having sex? No. But it's about time they know we sleep together at night. We're engaged to be married and they think of you as their daddy. Mommies and daddies sleep together at night. No more sneaking back to your room in the wee hours of the morning." I winked. "Now come on before you kill my mood."

We tiptoed down the hall, past my mom and Fred snoring in their room. I peeked in at Lucy and Piper as we passed.

"They good?" Brody whispered.

"Sound asleep." A seductive smile slid across my lips as I closed my bedroom door.

4

BRODY

"Brody. Brody," Kacie whispered loudly, her voice just strong enough to break into my nightmare of Viper covering me in feathers at my bachelor party. "Your phone is ringing."

I rolled toward her and grunted without opening my eyes, not yet fully awake.

"Brody!" She smacked my shoulder. "Wake up."

"Huh, what?" I sat up, trying to focus.

"Your phone is ringing. Again. It's rang like three times in the last twenty minutes."

"Oh." I reached for my phone and squinted at the screen. "It's my mom." I rubbed my eyes as I hit the button to accept the call. "Hello?"

"Do you have *any* idea how it feels to go to my monthly book club and have the ladies there tell me they read online that my only son is engaged? Let me tell you something, Mister, it feels really shitty!" my mom yelled into the phone.

Crap. She never yells. She never swears. Double whammy.

"Mom, I'm so sorry. We were gonna come by today and tell you," I lied, shrugging at Kacie, who was glaring at me now that she realized

I hadn't told my mom. "It just happened a couple days ago, and we've been so busy since then."

"Busy? You've been busy?" She drew out each word and emphasized each syllable.

Fuck.

"You're right." I sighed, feeling awful that I'd forgotten to call the one person who should have received the *first* call. "I can't tell you how sorry I am, Mom."

Kacie lay down and snuggled into me as I begged my mom for forgiveness.

"So," she sighed in defeat. "How'd you do it? Propose, I mean."

She was done yelling at me, but I could actually *feel* her sadness through the phone. I pictured her sitting at the kitchen table with a crinkled, tear-soaked tissue in her hand. My chest ached. Putting my hand over the phone so she couldn't hear me, I whispered to Kacie, "Do we have any plans today?"

She rolled onto her back and looked up at the ceiling, trying to remember. "No, I don't think so."

"Mom, what are you doing today?"

"Nothing, just some picking up around here, maybe a little weeding if the rain holds off."

"Remember when I was little, before we traveled for hockey all the time, and every summer we would go to the chocolate festival in Long Grove?"

"Mmhmm, that was always fun." Her voice sounded a little more upbeat at that memory.

"Well, it's this weekend. What if me, Kacie, and the girls come get you and we all go to that? Just like we used to, except now instead of you and your kid, it's me and my kids?" Kacie threw her arm around me and hugged me tight while I continued, "Then Kacie can tell you about the proposal in person while I feed Lucy and Piper so much chocolate their bellies will ache for a week."

"Brody," my mom said softly, "that sounds absolutely wonderful."

"Great! We'll pick you up in a couple hours?"

"Perfect." I could tell she was smiling now when she talked. "See you then."

Two hours later, we were in Kacie's Jeep, heading toward my mom's. I liked when Kacie drove. Her tanned legs reached out toward the pedals, the sun glistened off her copper hair as it whipped round and round her head, and don't even get me started on the way the seat belt sat so perfectly right in the middle of her breasts. With my sunglasses shielding my eyes, she had no idea I stared at her constantly. Sometimes I got so wrapped up in watching her movements, I forgot where we were going—and who we were with.

"Did you hear me?" Lucy squeaked from the backseat.

I turned to the side so I could hear her better. "I'm sorry, baby. What did you say?"

"What *is* Chocolate Fest?"

"Chocolate Fest . . . well, it is what it sounds like. Long Grove is this little town that's full of shops and restaurants and toy stores." Their faces lit up when I said "toy stores," but I just kept going. "During the festival, they close off all the streets and people set up different carts and they sell all sorts of chocolate desserts and chocolate-covered things. There are magic shows and dancers and pony rides. It's gonna be so much fun!"

Piper gasped. "Pony rides?"

"Yep, pony rides. Do you like ponies?" I asked.

"I love them." She sighed.

I looked over at Kacie, who glared at me out of the corner of her eye. "Absolutely not," she warned sternly.

"What?" I laughed innocently.

"I know you, Murphy. I know what you're thinking, and the answer is absolutely, one hundred and fifty percent no."

She called me Murphy. That has the same effect on me as when I say something about a barn to her.

"There she is!" Piper yelled as we pulled into my parents' property. My mom was standing on the porch, watering her flowers. When she saw us pull up the long driveway, she put the watering can down and waved at us.

Kacie parked her Jeep and we all hopped out as Mom made her way down the steps. Lucy and Piper ran right over and threw their arms around her waist, nearly knocking her down.

"Hi, girls!" She bent over and hugged them back. "How have you guys been?"

"Good," Piper answered.

"We're gonna live in a castle!" Lucy yelled in excitement.

My mom's head snapped up as her eyes darted back and forth between Kacie and me. "Something else you forgot to tell me?"

Kacie crossed her arms across her chest and cocked her hip to the side, staring at me. "Go ahead, big shot. Tell her what you did."

"I didn't do anything," I laughed, narrowing my eyes at her. "When we told the girls we were getting married, to make it easy for them to understand, I compared us to Cinderella and the prince."

"So then," Kacie piped in when I refused to tell any more, "they started dancing around and cheering that we're all going to live in a castle. I stopped them and explained that no, we won't be living in a castle, and all they had to do was look at him and . . ." She paused and motioned for me to finish.

"And I promised them a castle." I shrugged.

"Brody Michael!" my mom shouted. "You can't promise things like that to little kids. They're never going to forget it."

"Thank you," Kacie said to her, clearly feeling vindicated.

"You know me, I never think that far ahead. I'll figure something out. Just watch me." I waved off both of those skeptical women as I walked past them into the house. "I gotta take a leak real quick and then we'll go."

When I came back outside, Lucy and Piper were hanging upside down from the swing set my mom had put in. My mom and Kacie were sitting on the wicker couch on the porch, facing each other and holding hands.

Kacie had tears in her eyes. Mom's face was soaked. That couldn't be good.

"What . . . uh . . . are you guys okay?" I stuttered nervously.

When Mom heard me, her face instantly softened into a smile and she stood and walked over to me. She cupped my face in her hands. "My sweet, sweet, romantic boy. Kacie was just telling me about your proposal. Amazing, Brody."

I felt my face flush. "Thanks. I wanted it to be special for her."

"Well, I'd say you nailed it." She sniffed. "Let me run in and grab my purse."

Once she was inside the house, I looked at Kacie, who was wiping her eyes with a tissue. I smirked at her. "I sure did nail it that night, and I'm not just talking about the proposal."

"Brody!" she scolded quietly, looking toward the door to make sure my mom was gone.

"Sorry, I can't help it. I'm all revved up." I walked over and sat next to her on the couch, leaning in to kiss her neck.

"Chocolate festivals excite you that much?" She giggled.

"No." Kiss. "But." Kiss. "You called me Murphy." Kiss.

The wooden screen door creaked as my mom came back out. Kacie pushed my chest away from her, standing up quickly.

"I think I'm gonna drive separate, if that's okay?" My mom pulled her keys out of her purse as we followed her down the steps.

"Okay." I was confused. "How come?"

"Hey, guys!" my dad bellowed as he came out the front door. "Want me to lock this?"

"Yes, please," Mom called back.

I put my hand on my mom's arm and stopped her. "What's going on?"

She turned around and looked down at my hand and back up at me. "What?"

"Dad. Why is he here? You guys are divorced," I said, more accusatory than I meant to.

"Brody"—Mom's eyes searched my face as she sighed—"we were married for thirty years. Whether we're still together intimately or not, we're still friends and we still care about each other. He was here working in his shop. I told him we were going; he asked if he could join us." She stood up on her tippy-toes and kissed my cheek. "Simple as that. Now let's go."

She spun on her heel and started toward her car. Kacie hooked her arm through mine and yanked on it to get my attention. "Come on, *Murphy*." My eyes dropped to hers quickly and she winked at me, tugging me toward the Jeep. "Girls! You wanna swing all day or you wanna eat chocolate? Come on!"

The fair was hopping.

People everywhere. Chocolate everywhere. Games everywhere.

I kept my hat pulled low and sunglasses on so that I could enjoy the day with my family without being mobbed by fans.

The girls had already binged on chocolate-covered strawberries, chocolate-covered potato chips, chocolate-covered Rice Krispies Treats, and frozen chocolate-covered bananas, but they were still asking for more.

"Can we go over there?" Lucy pointed to a stand that sold chocolate-covered nuts and raisins.

"How can you guys possibly have any more room in those little bellies of yours?" my mom teased.

I looked out over the crowd and leaned into my mom. "Hey, would you do me a favor?"

"Sure."

I whispered in her ear and handed her some money.

"Lucy, Piper, come on. Let's go get something off that cart." My mom held out her hand, and she and Dad walked away with the girls.

Kacie started to follow them, but I reached out and caught her hand, pulling her in the other direction. "This way." She narrowed her eyes and frowned slightly in confusion but didn't argue.

The air smelled like chocolate and cinnamon as we walked hand in hand through the hordes of people stuffing their faces with food. The closer we got to our destination, the tighter Kacie squeezed my hand.

"Brody . . ." She tugged back hard, forcing me to stop and turn around. Her hands started to shake as she stared at the Ferris wheel behind me. "Don't make me do this."

"Come on. You can do it."

"No. I can't." She looked so tiny and terrified standing in front of me, hugging herself.

"Come on." I reached out and took her hands again. "You trusted me once. Trust me again."

She covered her face with her hands as a heavy sigh crept out of her. "Fine," she snapped, dropping her hands, "but I'm closing my eyes, and you can't bitch at me about it."

I laughed at her adorable tantrum and nodded. "You got it."

We got in line, and I stood behind Kacie, wrapping my arms around her waist just in case she got the idea to make a run for it. The Ferris wheel stopped, people started filing out of the exit, and we started inching forward. Kacie dug her heels into the ground and fought me, so I smacked her on the ass and she jumped ahead. "There we go. Now you're moving," I teased.

We got up to the ride attendant and I handed him our tickets.

"You want inside or outside?" I asked.

"What does it matter? If our basket breaks free and we tumble to the ground, we're both gonna die anyway," she barked.

"Way to be positive, babe," I joked, pushing her gently into the seat.

She sat, and I slid in next to her, lowering the bar over our laps. Once the attendant started the wheel to advance to the basket behind us, Kacie's hands flew up over her face again. I put my arm around her shoulder and pulled her into me, feeling a little guilty that she was so terrified while I was completely relaxed with her head on my shoulder.

A few more stops and our ride started spinning round and round. Kacie burrowed farther into the crook of my arm and hid her face like a squirrel does when it doesn't want to be seen. We were past the dock when the ride came to a stop, so I knew we'd have a few minutes before we got off.

"Hey," I whispered. "Where do you want to go on our honeymoon?"

Kacie loosened her grip on me a bit. "I don't know. I haven't really thought about it. Have you?"

"Not until we got on here."

She lifted her head a little and looked up at me, crinkling her brow and blinking in confusion. "Huh?"

"Your hair. It smells delicious—like coconuts—and makes me want to kidnap you to an island for a couple weeks."

Sitting up, she looked at me with wide eyes. "A couple weeks? Brody, the longest I've been away from the girls was two nights when we went for that quick weekend in Chicago. I don't know if I can do a couple weeks."

"That was a great weekend, wasn't it?" I growled softly as I stuck my nose in her hair again, taking a deep breath. "I think we set a new record for the number of times people can have sex in a two-day time span."

She giggled and leaned back into me. "That *was* fun. I think it took a week before I could walk right."

"Then let's do that again, but on some wonderful island with fruity drinks and white sand beaches," I suggested.

The ride jolted to a start again, and Kacie nearly jumped out of her skin, squeezing my hand so hard I thought she might break it. Once we stopped, she relaxed a bit. "Okay, let's do it. But . . . I can't do two weeks, Brody. It would be too much. I think a week is perfect."

"Deal."

"Are you mad?" I couldn't see her face, but her voice sounded concerned.

"No way." I shook my head. "As much as I want you all to myself, I get it. I'm gonna miss them too."

She squeezed me tight and leaned up, planting a kiss on my neck. "Thank you."

5

KACIE

Wedding planning was in full swing and I was on a roll.

Invitations picked out? Check.

Flowers picked out? Absolutely, mostly by Alexa, but she had fantastic taste.

Band picked out? Done.

The day I'd been most excited about was finally upon me. Wedding dress shopping! We had an afternoon appointment in the city at one of the most sought-after shops in all of the Midwest, but first my mom, Alexa, Lauren, and I were having lunch at the cutest little tea shop right down the street. Tea, scones, and chicken salad sandwiches were just what I needed to calm my nerves about finding a dress.

"I'm sorry again, guys," Lauren apologized for the twentieth time that morning as Max's hand barely missed the water glass he'd swung for.

"Lauren, stop it," I laughed. "It's really fine."

"I just had no idea that Tommy had agreed to work. I thought he'd be able to keep Max." She wiped the drool from his chin.

Reaching across the table, I scooped Max out of her arms and set him in my lap. "Are you kidding? I'm glad my godson gets to be here on wedding dress day. Let's just hope I can make a decision before he's walking, huh?"

"You'll be fine," Alexa said confidently. "Trust me, when you put it on, you'll just know."

"That's good, because right now I truly have no idea what I'm looking for." I sighed.

"And that's okay," my mom reassured me. "Like Alexa said, when you see it or try it on, you'll just know."

Alexa huffed and raised her water glass at me. "See? Alexa's always right."

"So, wait. Who's with the girls today?" Lauren reached over and handed Max his favorite plastic key ring.

Mom and I looked at each other and laughed, most likely thinking the same thing.

"Brody and Viper are babysitting," I answered nonchalantly, planting a bunch of kisses on Max's chubby cheek.

I looked up and Alexa's and Lauren's mouths both hung open as they stared at me blankly.

"What? Stop looking at me like that."

Alexa started to giggle while Lauren shook her head quickly. "Sorry, I'm just trying to picture Viper watching the girls, and the things that are popping into my head are scaring me."

That only made Alexa laugh harder. "Yeah." She took a deep breath, trying to compose herself. "They'll probably know how to spell the F word by the time you get home." She whooped louder than she had before.

I rolled my eyes. "Brody's there too. They'll be fine."

Am I trying to convince them, or myself?

We walked into Belle's Bridal, and it was like walking into a fairy tale. What the off-white walls lacked in color, the chandeliers, fancy chairs, and ambiance made up for ten times over.

A woman in her midthirties, who clearly had it all together, met us at the door. "Hello. Welcome to Belle's Bridal. How can we help you?" Her pale pink suit jacket and matching pencil skirt were completely wrinkle-free, and not one hair in her perfectly executed bun was out of place.

"Hi, we're a little early." My heart thumped nervously in my chest. The place was intimidating. "We have an appointment at two. My name is Kacie Jensen."

"Oh!" Her eyebrows shot up and her smile got a little wider. "*You're* Kacie Jensen." She said it like she knew who I was. "Come in, come in. It's so great to meet you. I'm Kate Porter, the store manager."

She extended her hand and I shook it happily.

I introduced her to my mom and my friends before she led us down a long hallway. The smell of roses filled the air, though I wasn't sure where it was coming from, and huge pictures of the most elegant brides I'd ever seen hung on the walls. She opened a big white door and stepped back, waving us in. "Come on in. This will be your private bridal suite for today."

We stepped in and I immediately loved the room.

"Wow! This is amazing!" My eyes darted around, wanting to look at everything all at once.

It was very different from the main part of the store, reminding me more of a trendy New York City loft than a bridal room. The walls were painted a cool, rustic shade of bluish gray and had funky artwork covering them. A white couch sat in the middle of the room, anchored on each side by hot-pink oversize chairs and a large, weathered coffee table in front. The whole setup faced a wall of mirrors that had a small stage in front of it.

We all filed in and were talking about the room when Kate picked up a phone on the wall. "Send Chloe in here, please."

About ten seconds later, a young girl appeared in the doorway carrying an envelope.

"Thanks, Chloe. Be on standby in case we need you." Chloe offered a smile before she nodded and walked away.

"I'm going to be assisting you today, with anything you need. Please, make yourselves comfortable." Kate motioned toward the seating area. We all shuffled over and sat down. "Before we begin, can I get anyone anything to drink? Sparkling water, champagne, a mimosa?"

"Oooo, I'd love a mimosa," Lauren said eagerly.

"Can I do a vodka and cranberry?" Mom asked.

"Sure thing." Kate nodded.

"Just water, please," Alexa groaned.

I laughed at her pouty face. "I'll just take water too, please."

"Kacie, you sure?" Mom questioned. "Have a cocktail if you want one."

"No, thanks. I need to be as sober as possible when I pick out a dress," I laughed.

Kate smiled. "Let me go grab those. I'll be right back. Feel free to start looking at some of the catalogs on the table, unless you already know what you're looking for." She winked.

"Okay, thank you." I leaned forward to pick up a magazine as she turned to leave the room.

"Oh, wait. I almost forgot. This is for you." She handed me the envelope and walked away quickly.

"What is it?" Mom sat up straight, craning her neck to see.

I shrugged, staring at my name on the envelope. "I have no clue."

Sliding my finger under the seal, I gently pulled to the side. Like a perfect envelope should, it popped open willingly.

I pulled out the folded piece of light blue paper.

Kacie,

Roses are red.
My jersey is white.
Pick any dress you want
for our big night.

Hey, babe. I hope you're having the best day with
your mom and friends. Like my award-winning
poem said, I've arranged everything with the shop in
advance. All you have to do is pick out your dream

dress, maybe something in a nice ice blue. ;) Have
fun! Love you!

Brody

"Oh my God." I rubbed the tears from my eyes and read the letter
again, hoping my brain wasn't playing a trick on me.

"What? What is it?" Lauren asked, gently rocking Max back and forth.

Unable to form a verbal response, I took a tissue out of my purse
and handed the paper to my mom.

She read it and gasped.

"Will someone read the damn thing out loud?" Alexa growled
impatiently.

Tears streamed down my face as my mom read the letter out loud.
It blew me away that not only had that crazy man called the salon and
arranged for the payment on my dress, but he actually took the time
out to write that note, and poem, and drop it off before I got there.

"Awww, that's the cutest thing I've ever heard." Lauren reached over,
grabbed a tissue from me, and dabbed at her eye.

"Wait. Ice blue? I don't get it," Alexa said, blinking quickly.

I thought back to that night and giggled. "Last year, we went to that
dinner party at Andy and Blaire's house, remember?" I cleaned the mascara out from under my eyes as they all nodded. "Well, I borrowed—"

"Yes!" Lauren pointed at me when she remembered, nearly dropping
Max in her excitement. "You borrowed that ice-blue dress from me."

"Yep, and he loved it . . . like . . . a lot." The look on Brody's face
as he stood in his kitchen said it all that night. I asked him what he
thought on a scale of one to ten. I would never, ever, ever, as long as I
lived, forget the number he said. Six hundred fifty-two.

"Obviously." My mom took Max from Lauren and bounced him
on her lap.

I took out my phone and texted Brody.

Hey. I just got the envelope. I can't believe you did that. Thank you, thank you, thank you!

Within seconds, my phone chirped.

B: I'm glad you liked it. You wouldn't believe how long it took me and Viper to come up with that damn poem.

Haha! Well, it made me laugh.

B: Good. I'd do anything for my girl.

And I would do anything for *YOU*! I love you so much!

B: I just sent you a pic. Remember how much you love me when you open it, okay?

Uh-oh.

The image came through, and I stared at the little hourglass spinning round and round, waiting for it to open. When it did, I squinted to get a better view. At first glance, the tiny image just looked like Lucy and Piper making silly faces, but when I blew it up with my fingers, it was a whole different picture. Their sleeves were rolled up and fake tattoos covered their forearms and biceps. They were both flexing, just like Viper was doing behind them, and they had their tongues sticking out. Brody had typed *Having fun with my tattooed Twinkies* above the photo.

"Oh my God." I started laughing so hard I could barely breathe.

"What now?" Mom looked at Alexa and Lauren, who just shrugged at her. Clearly, they all thought I'd lost my mind. Without saying a word, I handed my phone to my mom, who angled it so that Lauren and Lex could see too. Watching all of their faces when they saw my tattoo-covered twins only made me laugh harder.

"Well," Lauren finally said once we'd all finished laughing, "it's probably better than the F word, huh?"

Just then, Kate came back into the room carrying a silver tray with our drinks on it. "Who's ready to start looking at dresses?"

Three hours and twenty-seven dresses later, I found it. *The* dress. Lex and Lauren were right—I put it on and I just knew. I knew it was the dress I was supposed to walk down the aisle in. I knew it was the dress I was supposed to say vows to my fiancé in. I knew it was the dress I was supposed to dance with my husband in, and I knew it was the dress that would be tossed on the floor at the end of the night when I made love to that husband for the first time, officially.

Who knew drinking champagne and playing human Barbie all day could be so exhausting? When Mom and I got home, I was ready to collapse, but when you have two little girls excited to show you their tattoos, you have to play along.

"Mom! Mom! Look!" they both squealed, rolling their sleeves up as they ran to the front door.

"Oh my goodness, look at you two." I took turns inspecting each of their arms, which were completely covered in Hello Kitty and Teenage Mutant Ninja Turtles tattoos. "You guys got tattoos? Did they hurt?"

Piper covered her mouth with her tiny hands and giggled as Lucy corrected me. "No, Mom. They're not real!"

"Oh! Thank goodness." I wrapped my arms around both of them and pulled them against me. "I'm guessing you had fun with Brody and Viper today?"

"You mean Uncle V?" Piper pulled back and looked up at me.

"Uncle V?"

"Yeah, that's what he said to call him." Lucy shrugged, skipping off to the kitchen, with Piper trailing behind her.

"Uncle V got really into babysitting today, in case you couldn't tell," Brody joked as he came around the corner.

"Obviously." I met Brody halfway and melted into his open arms. I felt so tiny and safe and comfortable as I laid my head against his chest, I thought I could fall asleep right there, standing up. "Is he still here? I want to thank him."

"Nah, he left a while ago. Got a text from an . . . available female and off he went."

I rolled my eyes against Brody's chest and mumbled, "Available female, huh? Interesting word choice. I'll just text him later. Sounds like you guys had fun, though. I'm glad."

"I don't know how much fun Fred had." His laugh vibrated through me.

"Oh no, what happened?" I was too tired to lift my head and look at him.

"Well, he lost a bet. A big one. And Viper made him pay up."

"A bet about what? What did he have to do?" I groaned.

Brody rubbed my back and gave me one last quick squeeze before he released me. "He's in the kitchen. Go take a look."

As we walked toward the kitchen, I could hear my mom and the girls laughing. I turned and frowned up at Brody, who just looked down at the ground, trying to hide his grin. Nothing could prepare me for what I was about to see.

"What's going on? What's this big bet thing?" Fred's back was to me when I got to the kitchen, but as he turned slowly, I saw just what everyone was laughing at. Right there, smack-dab in the middle of Fred's forehead, was a Hello Kitty tattoo. "Uh . . . what . . . why?" I put my hand over my mouth, trying to hold it together, but it took about six seconds before I was laughing just as hard as the girls.

"I lost a bet." He frowned.

Brody walked up behind me and wrapped his arms around my shoulders, the perfect height for me to rest my chin and heavy head on. "We were talking about the nickname Twinkies, and that led to talking about the food Twinkies, and that led to Fred betting Viper he couldn't take down an entire box of Twinkies in two minutes. Viper doesn't turn down a bet—ever—so he ran to the gas station and bought a box. The rest, as they say, is history."

I shook my head back and forth in disbelief. "How long do you have to keep that on?"

"Just two days." Fred sighed. "But he's coming back tomorrow to take me to lunch. He's really rubbing it in."

I tapped Brody's arms so he'd let go. I needed some water. The girls were retelling the story to my mom in great detail as I grabbed a bottle from the fridge. "Wow. You guys are crazy." I laughed.

"Is this the mail?" Mom picked up the pile off the counter.

"Yeah, and Kacie, that huge pile over there is yours." Fred pointed.

"Really?" I was surprised. "I never get mail."

The stack of envelopes for me had to be two inches high. Once I started sifting through the stuff, I realized most of it was brochures from banquet halls and photographers, ring makers, and so on. One after the other, most of them with my name spelled wrong. "How did they even get my address?" I asked to no one in particular.

"I'm so sorry," Brody apologized as he watched me flip through the envelopes.

"Hey, stop it. This isn't your fault." I kissed his cheek as I continued flipping.

"Yeah, but I was afraid this would happen. As soon as word got out that we were engaged, I worried people would start hounding you. I should have warned you."

"I can handle some lame brochures. No biggie."

"Look, that one spelled your name right," he cheered, "and it doesn't look like a solicitation."

He was talking but I couldn't hear his words past the blood rushing in my ears. That one did spell my name right. It would've been pretty ridiculous if it had been spelled wrong.

That one was from my dad.

6

BRODY

Kacie was frozen like a statue, staring at the envelope in her hands. I lowered myself, trying to get a better view of her eyes. "Babe?"

She blinked but didn't respond.

"Kacie?" I asked again, my heart racing as I looked at the envelope.

"Honey, what is it?" Her mom took a couple of steps toward us as Fred and the girls turned too.

When Kacie still didn't answer, I slid the envelope out of her hands and took a closer look. "It's from Don Jensen?" I read the name out loud and looked up at Sophia. As I said the words, it hit me. Don was Kacie's dad's name. We hardly ever talked about him, but I remembered her mentioning it a couple of times.

Sophia moved in slow motion. Her hands crept up to her mouth as her eyes widened, staring at her daughter. Fred walked over and put his arm around Sophia's shoulders, pulling her from her moment of shock. She cleared her throat. "Are you gonna open it?"

Kacie's eyes moved from her mom's to mine. "I don't know. Should I?"

"I can't answer that for you, baby." I shrugged.

Reaching for the envelope, she took a big breath and ripped it open. I didn't want to rush her in case she didn't feel like reading it out loud, but from what I could see through the thin piece of paper, it wasn't a very long note. Sophia walked over to the fridge, opened the door, and started moving containers around, clearly trying not to stare at Kacie's reaction to the letter from her dickhead father, who'd walked out on them fifteen years ago. I'd obviously never met the man and shouldn't have been calling him names, but just knowing that he'd left his wife and daughter was enough of a reason for me. Shit, at this point I'd have a hard time walking away from Lucy and Piper, and they weren't even biologically mine. Speaking of them . . .

"Hey, what do ya say the three of us go in the living room and draw pictures of Fred with that tattoo on his head?" I had no idea what that letter said, or what was about to happen in that kitchen, but I felt like maybe the girls and I should go in the other room.

"I'm tired," Lucy whined.

"Me too." Piper yawned. "Can we just lie on the couch and watch *Frozen*?"

"Sure." I laughed, looking at my watch. "We haven't seen it in like five hours. You must be having withdrawal. Come on." Grabbing the bag of pretzels off the island, I led the girls to the family room.

The girls giggled at Olaf, the goofy talking snowman, as I kept my eyes on the kitchen. Kacie handed the letter to Sophia. It didn't take Sophia long to read it and set it on the island next to her, where Fred leaned in and read it over her shoulder.

"What are you gonna do?" Sophia asked, barely loud enough for me to hear.

Kacie tucked her hair behind her ear and shrugged as Sophia reached out and pulled her in for a hug. The second I heard Kacie sniffle, I slipped out from under the girls and told them I'd be right back. As I walked up behind Kacie, Sophia pursed her lips over her daughter's shoulder, transferring her to me when I got close enough. I wrapped my arms around her and hugged her tight as Sophia grabbed the letter and held it up for me to read.

Kacie,

Read about your engagement in the paper and realized
how much I've missed out on. I was hoping we could
do lunch and catch up. We have so much to talk about.

Love,
Dad

763-555-0616

"It's not that I don't want to see him"—Kacie straightened up suddenly, as if someone had asked her a question—"but why now? Why
today? I had the best day, and this just puts a dark cloud over it." She
sat down at the island and read the letter again.

"So don't meet up with him. You're not required to." I walked
behind her and started rubbing her shoulders.

"I know, but I would like to hear what he has to say. I have so many
questions. Where's he been living? How many brothers and sisters do I
have? Why did he have to leave *me* behind in the first place?" Her head
snapped up in Sophia's direction. "Sorry, I didn't mean it like—"

"Honey, you have nothing to apologize for. I made peace with your
father walking out years ago." She cupped Kacie's damp cheeks in her
hands. "If you want to call him, meet up, and start a relationship, you
have my blessing. If you want to throw that letter in the garbage and
pretend you never got it, you have my blessing on that too. I support
anything you decide."

"I know." She sniffed, staring down at the counter. "But he *is* my
dad. What if he's realized he made a colossal mistake and wants to try
and fix things?"

Fred's face twisted silently when Kacie used the word "dad." He was
being respectful and keeping quiet, but I knew that had to be a punch
in the gut for him. His eyes caught mine and I pressed my lips together
in a tight, sympathetic smile.

"You don't owe him anything. This is solely up to you. It's about what *you* want to do," Sophia responded.

"I wish I knew what I wanted, Mom. It's been so long since he's been gone, I don't even know what it feels like to have a dad anymore. I don't think I can pass this up."

"What if he's, ya know, contacting you for the wrong reasons?" I mumbled slowly. The words were barely out of my mouth and I already regretted them.

Kacie looked up at me with the most beautiful red-rimmed eyes. "What do you mean?"

"I don't know. His timing is a little convenient, don't ya think?"

"You don't even know him," she shot back.

"I just want you to be careful, Kacie. You don't know him either." I didn't mean to lecture her, but I'd seen people do things like this before. Unfortunately, even my own extended family had crawled out of the woodwork a time or two when they needed something.

She got up from the island and sighed as she walked over and plopped on the couch with the girls, pulling them to her side as she covered the three of them with a throw blanket.

"She mad at me?" I whispered to Sophia.

Sophia glanced past me to Kacie and shrugged. "I don't think so. I think you probably told her what she was already thinking and she didn't like it."

"You think so?"

"I meant it when I told her that I'd made peace with him leaving me, but that didn't mean my anger toward Don walking out on *her* ever went away. He could've still taken her on weekends and been involved in her life. I would've encouraged it." She nervously spun her wedding ring. "It was a struggle at times, but I really concentrated on never saying anything bad about him to her or around her. Still, I think even with me keeping my mouth shut, she knew he wasn't a good man. I'm sure this letter is a big red flag for her, but she's so desperate to mend fences, she's just not seeing it."

"You okay?" I looked up at Fred, who was sitting next to Sophia. He nodded quickly, taken aback by my question. "I'm fine."

"I know that was hard to hear—that part about wanting a dad. I think she's just stressed right now. She didn't mean it," I offered, trying to justify Kacie's choice of words.

"It's the truth. I'm not her dad and I can't take it personally that she wants to get to know him." He reached up and swiped at his eye, clearing his throat. "Doesn't change the way I feel about her."

A small smile crept across Sophia's face as she squeezed Fred's bicep and rested her head on his shoulder.

I turned around to peek at the couch. The girls were reciting the movie word for word. Kacie stared off into space, clearly distracted. I turned back to Fred and Sophia, tilting my head quickly toward the family room. "We have our cake tasting tomorrow. I hope she's talking to me by then. I'm as excited about that as she was about dress shopping."

Sophia chuckled and shook her head. "Oh, Brody, you're too much."

"Too much what?" Kacie came up behind me and hugged my waist.

I put my hands over hers and squeezed back. "I was just telling your mom how I'm skipping breakfast in the morning so I can eat as much Oreo cake as I want at Pearl's tomorrow."

Kacie gasped and flew around to the front of me, a huge grin displayed on her face. "Oh my God! I forgot we have our cake tasting tomorrow."

"Yep." I bent down and kissed her adorable crinkled nose. "I've already decided I'm voting for the Oreo one, but I'm still going along for all the free samples."

"Mom"—Kacie turned around to face Sophia—"I totally forgot. Are you able to watch the girls tomorrow?"

"We could always ask Uncle V," I joked.

"No." Fred frowned.

"Yes, I'm free." Sophia kissed Fred's forehead, right on the pink-and-white Hello Kitty. "Just bring me back some free samples, okay?"

7

KACIE

I never thought I'd say this, but I couldn't get to work fast enough. The last couple of months of wedding planning had been so hectic that the chaos of the hospital actually calmed me. Plus, I'd accepted a position in the labor and delivery unit, and this job definitely came with some perks. Something about holding a brand-new, minutes-old baby as his tiny pink body squirmed in my arms, and watching him open his eyes for the first time ever, just made all the problems outside of those four walls seem trivial.

It'd been two weeks since I received the letter from my dad, and I still hadn't decided what to do with it. Every time I made up my mind, within a couple of hours I had talked myself out of it. Brody's words kept ringing in my ears. He was right—I didn't know my dad at all. But what if . . . *what if* this was my shot at having a real relationship with my dad?

"Different department but the same glazed-over look on your face."

I knew that voice instantly, even before the wadded-up glove hit me in the side of the head. Turning to my right, Darla's smiling face greeted me.

"Hey! Long time no see." I rushed over and threw my arms around her neck. "I've missed your face."

She hugged me back quickly. "All right, enough, enough. You know feelings make me ill."

Refusing to let go, I giggled against her. "Nope. Not done yet. Deal with it." I really did miss working with her every day, more than I'd realized until that moment. After another minute, I released her.

"Ugh," she huffed. "I thought I was gonna have to have you surgically removed." She ironed out her scrubs with her hands.

I leaned against the counter and crossed my arms. "How have you been? How are things downstairs?"

"They're okay." She rolled her eyes, grabbing the bag of chips off the counter.

"Those aren't mine."

"Like I give a shit," she growled, shoving a chip in her mouth.

A happy sigh left my mouth. "I really have missed you. And your attitude."

We'd only seen each other a handful of times since I'd moved upstairs. Between different floors and opposite schedules, we barely even bumped into each other anymore, except for the one time last month she hid behind my car in the parking garage. Just as I got to my car and opened the door, she jumped out and scared me so bad that I literally peed my pants.

"Seriously." She glared at me midchew with a pile of chips in her mouth. "Knock it off. What happened to you? You got engaged and now you're Suzy Sunshine?"

"Pretty much." I laughed. "You gonna come to my wedding?"

"Depends when it is. My social calendar's pretty full," she answered dryly.

"You're such a brat. We both know you wouldn't pass up the chance to see Viper in a tux."

"Please." She threw her head back and laughed. "His clothes just get in the way."

I looked at my watch. "Aren't you getting off late?"

"Yeah, we were swamped down there this morning, but it's calm now. Huge construction accident brought six guys in with minor to moderate injuries." The chip bag crinkled as she shoved her hand in again. "I was really hoping one of them had a leg injury so I could take their pants off, but no dice."

"How can you possibly be walking around horny when you're together with Viper, the walking hard-on?"

"Whoa, whoa, whoa. Who said anything about us being together?"

"Then what are you?"

A Cheshire grin slowly crept across her face as she rolled her top lip in between her teeth. "We are simply two grown, consenting individuals who happen to enjoy each other's genitalia . . . and tongues."

"Uh . . . I think I came up here at the wrong time." Zach had rounded the corner, but stopped suddenly, throwing his hands up in front of him.

Darla and I looked at each other for a split second before bursting into laughter.

"You're fine. Come on over," I tried to say in between giggles as I sat down on my chair behind the nurse's station.

"What's up with you?" Darla asked Zach, turning on the charm. "Haven't seen you much lately."

He ran his hands through his dirty blond hair and let out a heavy sigh. "I know. I've been working so hard on trying to get this dependency program moving over in the east building. I've been begging for sponsors, trying to secure funding. The hospital is behind it, but there's a lot of politics involved, so I'm trying to do as much as I can on my own. In between that I'm trying to see the girls as often as I can. Oh, and there's that working thing that actually pays my bills." He laughed. "I try to do that as much as I can too."

"I'm proud of you." I smiled. "Once you get this thing up and running, it's gonna be great."

"Thanks. It'll be small to start, but baby steps, right?" He tapped his hands nervously on the counter. "I actually wanted to talk to you about the girls, if you have a second?"

"Yep." I took a quick peek at the monitors. "I only have two mommies and they're both sleeping."

"Before you start," Darla jumped in before Zach could talk, "I'm gonna head out." She blew me a kiss. "We'll catch up soon."

I blew her a kiss back and swiveled my chair to face Zach head-on. "What's up?"

"Funny you should say that, actually. My sister is up, from Kentucky. She just had a baby a couple months ago."

"Awww. Tell her I said congrats."

"I will." He nodded, his eyes darting all over the place. "Anyway, her and her husband came up with the baby and they're going to be here this weekend. I was wondering if I could have the girls overnight?"

I was happy with the place Zach and I were in. Over the last year, he'd visited with the girls a couple of dozen times, always at my house or he'd just take them out for the day. I hadn't been comfortable with him taking them to his apartment overnight, and up until this point, he'd let me drag it out, but I knew I couldn't dodge it forever.

Swallowing the selfish lump that had formed in my throat, I put on my most sincere fake smile and tried to sound as upbeat as possible. "Sure."

He tilted his head to the side and raised an eyebrow at me. "Thanks for that."

"No problem."

"No, not for letting me have them. Thanks for trying to sound happy about it."

Cringing, I covered my face. "I'm sorry. Was I that obvious?"

"Kinda." He laughed. "But I get it. It's okay."

I dropped my hands into my lap and looked up at him, feeling horrible. "It's not you. I'm just not used to being away from them."

"I know. I understand. If you're not comfortable with it, Kacie, we can just skip it."

"No," I insisted. "You've been a constant part of their lives for almost a year. It's time. I need to get over my issues."

His face flushed as he dropped his gaze to the ground. "Thanks. I appreciate it."

"Excuse me," a man's voice called out. "My wife just woke up and said the contractions are getting really bad. She wanted me to ask if you can check her?"

"Absolutely." I stood up and walked out from behind the desk area, whispering at Zach as I walked by, "We'll talk later, okay? But let's plan on that."

He nodded and thanked me again.

Fast-forward to Friday night and I was a nervous wreck. I'd packed, unpacked, then repacked the girls' bags four times just to make sure they had everything.

"Kacie, they're only going for two nights," Brody teased as he watched me rifle through the bags and pull everything out for the fifth time.

"I know, but I want them to be comfortable and have their stuffed animals and—"

"Babe. They're good." He walked over and took Lucy's pajamas out of my hand, gently tucking them back into her Princess Sofia duffel bag. "I know this is tough for you, but in the long run, as much as I hate to admit it, it's probably best for them," he said. I could see the tension in his jaw.

"Is this hard for you too?"

"Of course," he admitted. "Selfishly, I want them to love me more than Zach. I know he's their biological dad, but they're such an important part of me, it would sting like a motherfucker if they ever chose him over me."

I nodded and looked down at their duffel bags filled with four pairs of pajamas, stuffed animals, and toothbrushes.

"Kind of like it stung for Fred the other night," Brody continued slowly.

My head snapped up as my eyes bored into his. "Huh?"

"I watched him when you went on and on about that letter from your dad. He didn't say a word, but I know it must have been hard for him to listen to you talk about wanting a relationship with your real dad."

"Oh, it's different with Fred and me." I waved him off, not wanting to think for a minute that I'd hurt Fred's feelings.

"Really? How so?"

"For starters, I was twelve when we bought this place, and secondly, he wasn't even *with* my mom until a couple years ago."

"Get real." He took Piper's stuffed bunny out of the bag and threw it at me. "They may not have told *you* they were together, but those two have been going at it for years behind your back. And regardless of when they started seeing each other, he didn't have to be making out with your mom at night to care about you."

"I guess." I shrugged.

A knock on the front door cut our conversation short. I took a deep breath and puffed my cheeks out as I exhaled. "It's go time."

As we walked out of my room, the girls came flying out of theirs, racing each other to the front door.

"You got this, kid." He rubbed my shoulders, walking behind me.

"I'm opening the door!" Piper bounced up and down excitedly.

Lucy pouted, sticking out her bottom lip. "No, I wanna open it."

"I'm opening it."

I hushed both of them as I walked past, grabbing the knob and pulling it.

Zach's head snapped up quickly. "Hi," he greeted me nervously.

"Hey."

I tried to sound peppy, but I knew I was failing miserably. I'd had the girls almost solely to myself for the better part of the last five years, and I wasn't yet ready to share, but it had to be done. Like a Band-Aid, just rip it off.

Zach offered his hand to Brody, who didn't hesitate in shaking it. While those two would never be best friends, they'd been able to come to an understanding of sorts. Zach didn't interfere in or question Brody's role in the girls' lives, and Brody didn't try to stop Zach from starting a relationship with them. I felt so blessed that they were able to see past their pride and embrace what was best for Lucy and Piper.

"So, what's on the agenda this weekend?" Brody stood with his legs apart more than usual and puffed his chest out. While he wanted what was best for his Twinkies, every once in a while he still had to let his alpha flag fly just a little bit.

"My sister is in town with her husband and new baby girl. I think we're gonna take the kids to the zoo and maybe let them swim at the hotel pool. Nothing too exciting."

Pool? Oh my God. I hadn't even entertained the thought of them swimming.

"Zach, they've taken lessons, but neither of them are great swimmers yet." My voice squeaked as I felt the panic rising in my chest. Brody must have sensed it too and instinctively found my hand, squeezing it gently.

"You mentioned that before, so I went to the sports store and bought these really cool suits that have floaties built into the chest area and actually make it impossible for them to be submerged," he said proudly. "They can go down the slides and go under real quick, but they immediately pop right back up. They're pretty cool."

"Those *do* sound cool. We should get them for here too, Kacie." Brody did his best to sound reassuring.

Oddly enough, I didn't need it. Just knowing that Zach had thought ahead and taken the time to run to the store and get the girls something that would both protect them and satisfy my crazy overprotectiveness made me feel so much better. It also showed me just how much Zach had grown over the last year. In the beginning, it was rocky. He hadn't known them and they hadn't known him, but he'd done his best to try to learn all he could about them and have fun every time he was over.

But now, this showed me he was thinking like a real dad. In that moment, I relaxed. Maybe my relaxation would last five minutes, maybe five days, but I knew Zach was capable of being a great father to them. With him and Brody behind them, Lucy and Piper were gonna conquer the freaking world.

8

BRODY

"How you doing?"

Kacie sighed and let her head fall back against the couch, turning it to look at me. "Miserable."

I pushed a stray piece of hair from her forehead. "For what it's worth, you make miserable look beautiful."

She smiled at me and leaned over, resting her head on my shoulder. "Thank God I have you here with me or I'd lose my mind."

"I know." I squeezed her knee gently. "You're doing good."

I lied. She wasn't doing that great, but some lies are just necessary. Lucy and Piper had only been gone two hours and she'd already texted Zach twice to check on them. I had to give the guy credit, though, he was being very patient with her.

"How long have they been gone?" she whined.

My head fell against the couch, mirroring hers. "About ten minutes longer than the last time you asked."

She grimaced. "No way am I going to make it."

"Yes, you will." I stood up and grabbed her hands, pulling her up too. "Come on. I wanna show you something."

"Where are we going?"

I pulled her along behind me, out the front door. "Hush. You'll see."

Holding the passenger-side door of my truck open while she hopped up, I stood back and whistled for Diesel, who was sound asleep on Kacie's porch. "Come on, you lazy bastard." He opened his eyes and slowly walked down the steps and over to my truck. I stared down at him and he stared up at me. "Well, come on. Get up there," I ordered. Two steps back, one running start forward, and he leaped into the backseat of my truck, parking comfortably in the middle of the two booster seats in the back.

I walked around to my side of the truck and climbed up, smiling at Kacie, who was looking at me out of the corner of her eye.

Shooting her a big, cheesy grin, I started the engine and pulled out of her driveway. After driving north for fifteen minutes or so, she asked again, "Are you gonna tell me where we're going?"

"I want to check on something and figured you might want to see it too."

That answer appeased her for the rest of the ride as we held hands in silence, with Kacie checking the time on her phone every ten minutes or so.

A little while later, we pulled into my parents' farm. The gravel popped and leaves crunched under my tires as I drove the truck all the way up past the house and to the left, where vehicles didn't usually go.

"What are you doing?" Kacie exclaimed.

"You'll see." I winked at her.

I steered the truck carefully around my dad's shop and past some tall grass until the barn came into view. Kacie grinned when she saw it, still with *Will You Marry Me? #30* painted in red on the side. While the rain had faded it a tad, it wasn't gone completely. I hoped it never would be.

"What are we doing here?"

Parking the truck, I jumped out and went around to her side to open the door. "Come on out and you'll see."

Diesel almost knocked her over as he jumped out and chased a flock of geese into the lake, which was tinted orange from the setting sun. Kacie checked her phone one more time and took my hand. We walked up to the barn doors and I turned to face her. "I have no idea what it's going to look like in here, but I had a crew come out the last two days. They've been cleaning out all the old hay and cobwebs and stuff."

Kacie's lips curled into a wide smile as she bounced up and down excitedly, clapping her hands.

Laughing at her reaction, I pushed the heavy door open and propped it so we had as much light as possible. The barn looked fantastic, better than I had imagined.

"Oh my God." Kacie's mouth hung open as she walked wide-eyed around the first floor of the barn. Every corner, every nook, had been swept and wiped completely spotless. Not one piece of hay or one speck of dust was visible. "This looks incredible."

"It does." I was pleasantly surprised as I wandered the first floor too. "They even cleaned the windows."

"This is gonna look so pretty, Brody."

I was happy to hear joy back in her voice. It was an added bonus that she hadn't looked at her phone in a few minutes.

"It is. Where do you want to put everything?" I had no idea how this was actually going to work.

"I'm thinking the band will go over here in this corner so they don't take up too much floor space." She walked from the corner over to the far wall with the window above it, which was missing half its glass. "And I think the head table will look good here."

"What's a head table?"

"It's where the bride and groom eat with their wedding party, but I'm pretty sure Alexa and Lauren are going to want to sit with Derek, Tommy, and Max, so we might switch it up and just have you and me. What do you think?"

"I'm thinking we make it a table for four and have it be you, me, and the Twinkies. What do *you* think?"

"Brody." She tilted her head to the side as her eyes focused on mine softly. "I think that's incredibly sweet. They're going to think they are so cool sitting up front with us."

"It'll be our first official family dinner. We have to be all together."

Kacie swallowed hard and sighed. "I still ask myself every day what I did in a previous life to deserve you, and I'm convinced I must have saved a bus full of children and puppies from falling off a cliff onto a senior citizen home or something."

"Super Kacie. Got a nice ring to it, don't ya think?"

"More like Super Brody." She walked over and tucked her arms under mine, resting her head on my chest. Our hug didn't last long as a loud chirp came from Kacie's back pocket. She took her phone out and squinted to see the screen better. "Awww," she cooed. "Look."

She turned the phone my way. It was a picture of Lucy and Piper holding their new baby cousin.

"That was nice of him to send that," I said sincerely.

She nodded, still staring at the picture. "Yeah, it was. He's really trying, isn't he?"

"He sure is."

"Are you okay . . . with all of this?" She bit her lip nervously.

"Honestly, I was nervous at first, but he really seems to be making an effort with the girls and with you. As long as he keeps that up, I have no problem with him."

"You know," she murmured as she wrapped her arms around my waist again, "there is one *big* bonus to Zach taking the girls from time to time."

"Oh yeah?" I reached down and grabbed her butt, squeezing gently. "I'm liking the way this sounds, Jensen. Go on."

"It does allow us a little, uh, alone time in the evening. Something we don't get often."

"This is true, and if we can keep scheduling Zach's days with the girls on my off days, that'll work out *real* nicely."

Hockey season was back in full swing, but Kacie and I had gotten very good at making use of the time we had together. She and the girls had even started traveling with me every so often when they were off school or it was close enough to do a quick weekend trip.

She was rising up on her tippy-toes, her lips less than an inch from mine, when her phone chirped again.

"Okay, if he's going to text you every two minutes, I might have to kill him," I groaned as she reached for her phone.

Kacie's mouth fell open as her eyes read left to right quickly.

"What is it?" I craned my neck to peek over the top of her phone.

"It's Derek. Alexa's in labor—a month early. Come on. We gotta go."

I drove as fast as I could back to Pine City. More specifically to Rogers Memorial Hospital, where Kacie worked and Alexa was in labor. One perk of being engaged to a labor and delivery nurse was she knew right where to go when we got there. She practically sprinted through the halls and the double doors.

"Erica, what room is Alexa Harmon in?" she asked a woman in scrubs sitting behind the nurses' station.

"Kacie!" Derek called out from the end of the hall.

Kacie didn't wait for Erica to answer her, she just jogged straight to Derek. "How is she? What are they giving her to slow the contractions? Terbutaline?"

He put his hands up, halting her, both from running past him and talking. "They couldn't stop it. He's here. He came fast; she almost had him in the elevator."

Kacie's hands flew to her mouth as her voice cracked. "Him?"

"Yep. Joseph Derek Harmon. He weighed five pounds, three ounces. She's holding him now, but he won't eat yet."

"Sometimes their latch is undeveloped this early. He'll get the hang of it." Kacie sniffed as a tear rolled down her cheek.

I held my hand out to Derek. "Congrats, Dad."

He smiled as big as anyone I'd ever seen when he shook it. "Thanks. He's pretty damn awesome, even for being an hour old. I think he's a genius."

"Ha! First-time dads." Kacie rolled her eyes playfully. "Tell her I'm coming in." She pushed Derek back toward his room.

"Okay." He laughed. "But the doc said no visitors until we're in our real room."

"What doctor?"

"Dr. Newman."

Kacie waved Derek off. "Tell her it's me and she just delivered my best friend's baby. She'll let me in."

Derek stuck his head in the room and had a brief conversation with the doctor before pulling the door open. "She said fine, but just for a minute."

Kacie looked back at me and grinned, elated to go meet Joseph.

I followed her into the room. The lights were dim and soft music played quietly as a nurse scurried about cleaning things up.

"Congratulations." I walked over and kissed Alexa on the forehead.

"Thanks, Brody." She smiled up at me, rocking that new mom glow I'd heard about. I walked over and tucked myself against the wall, out of the way.

Kacie walked up and squeezed Alexa's shoulders. "Only you would look this good immediately after having a baby. Bitch."

Alexa laughed, then held her stomach and groaned. "I'm glad I look good, because I feel like shit. Why didn't you tell me my vagina was going to rip in half?"

Dr. Newman shook her head and looked at Kacie over her glasses. "She didn't even have an episiotomy."

Kacie glared at Alexa and rolled her eyes. "Drama queen." She walked over to the sink, rolled up her sleeves, and washed her hands and forearms, itching to get her hands on that baby.

"Gimme, gimme." She giggled as she scooped him out of Alexa's arms. "He looks *so* good, Lex. Not very jaundiced yet either."

Kacie gently swayed back and forth with the tiny white-and-blue blanket in her arms. She dipped her head and closed her eyes as she rubbed noses with Joseph. I stood in awe, staring at her as she fell in love with that baby right before my eyes. Surprisingly overcome with emotion, I could suddenly imagine our whole future, except it would be our baby she would be cradling and rubbing noses with. She was already the most amazing mom on the planet, and I couldn't wait to make her a mother again.

9

KACIE

I was nervous.

Not I-hope-I-make-it-on-time nervous or even please-don't-let-this-cop-pull-me-over nervous. I was interview-at-a-job-I-really-want, first-day-at-a-new-school, and about-to-take-my-state-boards nervous, all rolled into one.

It was the dead of winter in Minnesota, temperatures were barely in the double digits, and I was freezing my ass off sitting on a wrought-iron bench, but I just wasn't quite ready to go into the coffee shop and see my dad. You would think that after all that time, no matter what the circumstances of his leaving were, I'd be excited to see him, but I wasn't. I was terrified.

What if I didn't like him?

What if he didn't like me?

What if I lost the courage to ask him everything I'd wanted to ask him over the last fifteen years?

You know how you'll find out, Kacie? Go inside.

I don't know if it was my brain or my cold toes talking, but something willed me to start walking up the concrete steps and into the tiny green shop. A bell above the door clanged as I pushed it open. Soft music, warm air, and the smell of coffee immediately filled my senses, making me feel cozy and at ease. Maybe this would be a great day after all.

I took my coat off, intentionally not looking around at the tables. I don't know why, but I wanted him to see me first. As I moved in slow motion to hang my coat on a hook behind the door, I took a deep breath. Everything would be different when I turned around. Good or bad, it would be different.

One more big breath, and . . . turn.

My eyes scanned the restaurant, but I didn't see him. What was that feeling in my stomach? Disappointment? Relief? I wasn't quite sure, but something was weighing me down like a rock. A man in the far corner caught my attention as he stood up and waved at me.

Him.

My stomach flipped again as I smiled and waved back. I scooted past tables and chairs, trying to figure out what I was going to say to him. Thankfully, I didn't have to think for long. He went first.

"Kacie. Wow! Look at you," he boasted as I got closer. Walking around the side of the table, he held his arms out. I wasn't sure I was ready for a hug, but there was no going back now. As his scruffy cheek brushed mine, the smell of his aftershave instantly transported me back in time twenty years to when I would get a giant hug before he tucked me into bed every night. It was amazing how people could smell the same year after year.

"You're so beautiful," he said as he hugged me tight.

"Thanks," I offered back awkwardly. I pulled away and set my purse down in an empty seat, opting to sit across from him.

He settled into his seat too and took a cleansing breath. "So . . ."

"So." I smiled politely. "Great weather we're having, huh?"

My dad's deep laugh echoed throughout the quiet little coffee shop, a little too loudly. "Oh, Kacie. You always were quite the jokester."

What? No, I wasn't.

I never joked much at all. I was actually the opposite. I was the weird kid who made my bed every single morning and made sure my stuffed animals were lined up perfectly, in alphabetical order, of course. I was also the weird kid who brought carrots and snap peas to school in her lunch every single day. I was the weird kid who wouldn't swim for thirty minutes after eating for fear that I'd get a cramp and die in the lake. Joking was never my thing. That's why Brody and I got along so well. He was the jokester, the yin to my yang.

"Can I get you something?" The waitress's voice pulled me from my daydream and I stared up at her like she'd just asked me if I wanted to jump off the roof of the building. Her eyes darted to my dad, then back to me. "Ma'am?"

"Oh, I'm sorry." I shook my head to clear my thoughts. "I'll take a hot chocolate, please. Extra whipped cream."

"Sure thing. Be right back." She smiled kindly and walked away.

"How's your mom?"

I was surprised by my dad's first question, but my mom was a source of comfort and strength in my life, so I knew we couldn't go wrong there.

"She's great. Amazing, actually."

"Good to hear." He nodded. "Where's that superstar fiancé of yours? Thought maybe he'd be joining us."

"Nope. They have a home game tonight, so he's in the city."

"Oh." He sounded disappointed. "Do you go to a lot of his games?"

"As many as I can when I'm not working. I-I'm a nurse now," I added, realizing he knew nothing about me.

"Really? Good for you." He grinned proudly.

"Anyway, the girls and I love going—" I paused. "Do you know I'm a mom?"

His eyes went wide and his mouth fell open just a smidge. "No. I'm a grandpa?"

Resentment filled all my available head space when he called himself a grandfather. They already had two grandfathers—Fred, who'd been there for all their skinned knees and runny noses, and Bob, who'd made them the most adorable hot-pink mini picnic table for their birthday this past summer. He'd even stenciled their names and little white daisies on the corners of the benches. *That* was a grandfather.

"Yeah, you are. Twice, actually, in a matter of ten minutes." I chuckled nervously. "I have twin girls. They're six, almost seven."

"No kidding. That's amazing." He shook his head back and forth slowly. As I watched him talk, I started realizing I got more than just my reddish-brown hair from my mom. My dad had a large nose that leaned slightly to his left at the bridge and a square face, two things I was grateful I didn't win in the DNA lottery.

"I actually brought pictures of them." Reaching into my purse, it took me a minute, but I dug out half a dozen photos of the girls and set them on the table. "Their names are—" When I looked up from my purse, my dad had his phone up in front of him, and he was typing something.

"Oh, sorry." He fumbled to put his phone away when he realized I'd stopped talking. "What are their names?"

"Lucy and Piper." A small sigh left my body as I told him their names. "I have more pictures of them on my phone if you want to see them, tons of them." I laughed.

He picked the photos up and looked at them very briefly before dropping them back on the table. "They're cute. That's okay, you can show them to me another time."

"Okay." I was annoyed as I gathered up the pictures and put them back in my purse.

"Listen, I know it took three letters to get you here, but I'm glad you finally came. I want to talk to you about something." He lifted the red mug to his mouth and took a sip of his coffee. "I never read the newspaper anymore. Like most people, I get my news on the computer, but that one morning in June, for whatever reason, I happened to pick it up and there it was, right on the cover. My baby girl engaged to Minnesota's golden boy. It was perfect timing. A sign, if you will. Like someone was telling me it was finally time to get in touch with you."

I leaned back in my chair and crossed my arms over my chest, silently trying to figure out where he was going with this speech.

"Anyway, earlier that morning I had just been turned down for a business grant, and I think it might actually be a great investment opportunity for you."

My heart sank and my mouth dropped open.

"Well," he continued when he saw my reaction, "for you *and* Brody. You see, I'm trying to start a small consulting business, but I need the start-up money, so here's what I was thinking—if Brody could give me fifty grand up front, we can work out a percentage that he would get back annually. I was thinking maybe three percent? It's negotiable. With my money expertise and his cash to get it off the ground, I figure the business should really take off, and I can have him paid back in no time. He can be the silent partner in my little adventure. What do you think?"

Quietly, I closed my mouth and inhaled deeply through my nose, just staring at him. As his words sank in, the few fond memories of him I'd protected like gold since childhood faded away. All I would ever remember was that after fifteen years, my father finally contacted me because he wanted money—from my fiancé.

I was nothing but a rung on his slimy ladder. One he was going to use to get wherever he wanted.

"KJ?"

The instant he used the nickname he called me as a kid, I lost it.

"*This* is why you called me here? For money?" I hissed across the table, leaning forward.

"Well, I—I—I wanted to know what was going on with you too," he stammered. "I just think we should strike now while the iron is hot and run with this."

"Oh my God, you're unbelievable!" I jumped up, nearly bumping right into the waitress who was carrying my hot chocolate.

"Listen, the boy can't play hockey forever, Kacie. Get real." He smirked smugly, completely missing why I was upset. "He's going to need something to do after that. Why not invest wisely?"

"He *is* investing wisely. In me and my daughters. Life isn't just about money, *Don*. It's about family, and love, and living."

"That's naive. Sit down and let's get us both to a point where we can benefit from this."

His disgusting words dripped off of me and I suddenly wanted a shower.

"You sit there. I'm going home—to my *real* dad." I spun around and grabbed my coat, hurrying out the door before I could even put it on.

I felt like such an idiot as I rushed to my Jeep.

How could I have been so dumb?

Why on earth did I think a man who'd walked out on his family the way he did could have a sudden change of heart and want a relationship again?

Then it hit me—because Zach did. Zach had walked out just like my father had, but as it turned out, he *had* grown up and changed. He'd proven it every chance he got over the last year. Part of me was hoping for that same miracle in my dad, but instead, history had repeated itself. The only difference was this time I was old enough to understand what was *really* going on, and because of that, *I* was the one who walked out.

By the time I got home, tears were streaming down my face. I was so grateful the girls would still be at school for a couple more hours. Once in the kitchen, I realized no one appeared to be home. Then I remembered my mom had taken up a spin class on Tuesday mornings.

The house was quiet.

Too quiet, leaving me with nothing but my mind, which had chosen to replay the last couple of hours over and over again.

Don't be naive. Sit down. Get real.

Every time I thought about the words he'd said to me, my chest got tighter and tighter. I walked over to the couch in the family room and sat down slowly, determined not to let one more tear fall because of my dad. I just felt so . . . stupid.

"Honey, you okay?" Fred's gruff voice from the kitchen caught me by surprise. I'd been so lost in my own head, I hadn't even heard him come in. "What is it?" His eyebrows drew together as soon as he saw my face, and he rushed over. Sitting down next to me, he pulled me in close. That one hug from Fred was all I needed to completely come undone. Rocking me back and forth gently, he didn't ask another question. He simply let me cry it all out.

After a short eternity, I pulled back and sniffed.

Holding his index finger up in the air, he hopped off the couch. "Hang on." He rushed over to the bookshelf on the other side of the room and grabbed the box of Kleenex.

I took a tissue from him and blew my nose loud enough to scare the fish in the lake. "Sorry if I snotted on your shirt."

Fred looked down at his shirt and shrugged. "Don't worry about it. I like you, and your snot."

"I went to see my dad," I blurted out.

"Oh." A dazed look spread across his face as he nodded slowly. "How did that go?"

"It was awful." I started rambling. "He didn't ask one question about me. He didn't seem at all interested in anything I've been doing with my life. I tried to show him a couple of pictures of Lucy and Piper, and he barely even looked at them. Turns out he only asked me there so I would ask Brody to invest in some company he's trying to start."

"Seriously? That's horrible." Fred sounded even more outraged than I was. "How could he not look at those little girls and instantly fall in love with their sweet faces? How could he not be proud of you and all you've accomplished, almost completely on your own? Boy, that really pisses me off."

I looked up at Fred rubbing his clenched jaw with his worn hands. His eyes were angry. Angry and protective that someone hadn't given me and my daughters the attention he felt we deserved. Angry and protective the way a *real* dad would be.

"Fred?" I tried to speak past the golf-ball-size lump in my throat. "I'm so sorry for what I said the day I got his first letter . . . about wanting to finally have a relationship with my dad."

"It's okay, kiddo." He reached out and patted my knee. "I know how bad you've wanted a dad your whole life."

I stared deep into the beautiful sky-blue eyes of the man who'd taken me to the hospital for stitches in my chin when I was twelve and rode my bike straight into a tree. The eyes of the man whose silhouette had stood in the front window when Zach dropped me off from our first date. The eyes of the man who'd cried in front of me for the first time the day I brought the girls home from the hospital and he held one in each arm. The eyes of a man who didn't share one drop of blood with me, but loved me unconditionally regardless, when another man decided I wasn't worth it.

"That's just my point—I already had one. You're the best dad I could've ever asked for." Tears stung my eyes again, but these were happy tears. "We may not share blood, but we share more memories in one day than I had in ten years with him. You've been by my side as far back as I can remember, Fred, and it's just fitting that you be by my side on my wedding day. Would you please walk me down the aisle?"

"Wow." Fred swallowed and cleared his throat. "I'm sure glad that you feel that way about me, Kacie, because that's exactly how I feel about you. I would love to escort you down the aisle, right into the arms of the man who loves your girls the way I love you."

I threw my arms around his shoulders and squeezed as hard as I could. "I love you too . . . Dad."

10

BRODY

I liked to think of myself as a pretty even-keeled guy. Dealing with a lot of trash talk and bullshit on the ice had really numbed me to the dickheads of the real world. But one thing that sent me into attack mode was seeing someone I loved get hurt. Especially if that someone happened to be my fiancée.

"That sucks. What a prick." Andy sat in amazement as I told him the story of Kacie's meeting with her dad.

"Dude, she was so upset when she told me all of this last week, I wanted to find him right then and ring his fucking neck with my bare hands."

"I can imagine. Nothing worse than when someone makes your girl cry." He stood up, walked over to his printer, and removed the paper. "You really think this is gonna work?"

"It has to." I shrugged. "I know how people like him work. They only see one thing."

Andy made small talk for the next half hour while I eyed my watch and paced nervously around his office.

"Calm down." He laughed, sitting relaxed as ever at his desk.

"I just want to get this over with." I stretched my arms up high in the air, trying to relax myself any way I could. "Does nothing ever rattle you? You're the same person all the time."

"Sure, things get to me," he said nonchalantly, "but not dealing with scum like this."

Ellie's voice rang out in the room: "Mr. Shaw, your eleven o'clock is here."

Andy's eyes locked on mine. "Ready?"

"Fuck yes."

He pushed a button on his phone. "Thanks, El. Send him in."

A minute later, his office door opened and Ellie ushered in Don Jensen. I sat against Andy's desk, gripping the wooden end so tight I thought I might break it off. Andy sensed my tension and walked over to shake his hand first. "Hi, Don. Come on in."

Don finished with Andy and walked over to me, holding his hand out eagerly, completely oblivious when I ignored it. "So, this is the man engaged to my little girl. Congratulations, she's quite the catch."

How the fuck would you know?

"Hold my calls for a bit please, Ellie," Andy called out. Ellie nodded and shut the door behind her.

"Have a seat, Mr. Jensen." Andy waved toward his seating area.

"Please, call me Don." He grinned as he sat down, looking back and forth between me and Andy. "I was surprised to hear from you, Brody. Kacie left the coffee shop all huffy, but I'm glad she finally came to her senses and talked to you about my offer."

"Oh yeah, she talked to me about it," I said sarcastically. "It's like this, Don. I'm in love with Kacie. I love her more than I've ever loved anyone on this planet, and when someone upsets her, I will go to the ends of the earth to make sure that doesn't happen again. So here's the deal: Kacie doesn't want to see you again—ever—but I'm not stupid; I know how you people work."

His cheerful grin faded and was replaced with a frown as he realized he wasn't there for pleasantries.

"You sent her a letter. She ignored it, and you sent her two more until she finally agreed to come and meet you." I stood tall, crossing my arms over my chest. "So, here's what I'm proposing. She said you asked for fifty grand. I'm gonna double it and give you a hundred."

His eyes grew wide but he didn't respond, knowing I wasn't done.

"However, in order to get that hundred grand, you're going to sign the contract my good friend Andy is holding, promising that you will never, ever, ever contact Kacie, her daughters, or Sophia again or I will sue the shit out of you for twenty times what I gave you."

"And if I refuse?" he snarled.

"Then you leave here with no money, but still the same chances of getting near Kacie. I'll hire a security detail for her and the girls that'll give the president's a run for his money if I even *think* you're contemplating contacting her again. Money or no money, you'll never see her again."

"What are you, in the mafia?" he huffed.

"Nope." I raised my chin in the air. "I'm a lovesick man who has more money than he knows what to do with and will protect what's his at all costs."

"More money than you know what to do with?" Tilting his head to the side, a calculating smile crossed his lips. "Then I want more. Make it a million and you have a deal."

I stared him straight in the eye. "Go fuck yourself. Hundred grand, that's it. Take it or leave it, but you have two minutes to decide. Then I'm throwing you out on your ass, without a penny."

His eyes looked down at the ground as he contemplated his next move, even though I already knew exactly what it would be.

"Got a pen?" He sighed, glaring at Andy.

"Sure thing." Andy laid the contract on the coffee table in front of him and handed him a pen. He didn't even read it. He just signed his name as I took out my checkbook. I gnashed my teeth as I wrote the check. It wasn't about the money. That meant nothing to me. When Kacie cried as she told me about their meeting and how stupid her dad made her feel, my protective instincts took over and I knew I had to keep him away from her.

"You have the contract?" I asked Andy.

"Signed and dated," he confirmed.

"Here." I handed the check to Don, who grinned as he looked down at it. "Now get out."

Looking up at me, his smile grew bigger. "You don't have to tell me twice. Nice doing business with you boys." He nodded and turned toward the door. It would have been worth it to punch him right in the back of his smug head if I weren't still on probation for my bar fight incident.

The door closed and I slammed my palms down on Andy's desk. "He didn't even fucking care. How is that possible?"

Andy pressed his lips together in a tight line and shrugged. "I have no idea, man. No amount of money you offered or security team you hired would keep me away from my daughter, money or no money."

"You know what's sad? I would've paid the million without even thinking about it."

Andy's eyebrows shot toward the ceiling. "You would've?"

"Yep." I nodded. "In a heartbeat, but he was too desperate."

Andy clapped my shoulder and walked around behind his desk, filing the contract in a folder. "I can't decide if you're completely heartless or if you have the biggest heart in the world, Murphy."

"Don't go soft on me now, Shaw." I laughed for what felt like the first time since Kacie had told me about that meeting with her dad.

He sat down in his chair and rested his chin on his hands. "You gonna tell her you talked to him?"

"Nope." I didn't even hesitate with my answer. "She told me she never wanted to see him again, and I made sure that's going to happen. The details of how I went about it aren't necessary."

"I think Don was right." He laughed, shaking his head at me. "Maybe you *are* in the mafia."

11

KACIE

Like an impatient child, I'd wished the months away because I was ready to be Mrs. Brody Murphy approximately three minutes after he proposed, but now that our wedding was less than two weeks away, I wanted time to slow down so I could enjoy every second of it.

"Hey, sleepyhead." My mattress dipped as my mom sat down on my bed, gently brushing the hair from my face.

"Good morning," I moaned as I stretched out.

"So, I know you're busy with last-minute wedding stuff, but the girls and I were hoping we could steal you for a couple hours to go to the spa, get a mani-pedi, and maybe a facial if there's time. What do ya say?"

"I say that sounds fantastic." Sitting up in bed, I covered my mouth as I yawned.

"Good." She patted my knee. "Get moving. You have an hour."

An hour? I'd have to hurry. I hustled into the girls' bedroom to get their clothes out. "What do you guys want for breakfast?" I asked as I sorted through their messy drawers.

"Cinnamon rolls," Lucy said.

Piper frowned. "Chocolate chip pancakes!"

I stood up and sighed. "How about eggs?"

They both nodded in unison as I tossed two sundresses to them and hurried off to the kitchen. In record time, I had the pan on the stove and eggs scrambling while I threw a few bites of yogurt and granola into my mouth. Lucy's and Piper's cheery but sleepy little faces appeared in the kitchen the same time as my mom.

"Here ya go." I scooped some eggs onto two plates along with a handful of blueberries and set them in front of the girls.

Mom, who was already showered and ready to go, sat down next to them.

I scooped her up a plate of eggs too. "Since you're already sitting here, would you mind keeping an eye on them for a minute? I want to run and take a quick shower."

"Of course not. Go get ready." She waved me off.

A little while later, I threw on my favorite capris and Minnesota Wild T-shirt, tucked my damp hair into a neat braid, and went out to the kitchen.

The girls were sitting at the island, and my mom was leaning over them, whispering quietly.

I snuck up behind Lucy and Piper, reaching out and grabbing their waists as I got close. "What are you doing!" I yelled, scaring them half to death.

Piper screamed and giggled while Lucy whined, "Mooooom, did you hear our secret?"

"No." I stood up straight, looking at my mom suspiciously. "What secret?"

"Nothing," she snapped quickly. "Now leave it alone and let's go."

We piled into my mom's car and headed five miles or so down the road to Lavender and Lilies, a cute little spa in town that used to be an old house but had now been updated and converted into an intimate, relaxing assortment of rooms for pampering. Once inside the front door, a cute college-age girl sitting at a beautiful antique desk greeted us.

"Good morning." She smiled brightly, making eye contact with each of us. "How can I help you?"

"Hi." My mom stepped forward a bit. "We have appointments this morning, for all four of us."

"Great. What's the last name?"

"Jensen?"

"I have you down for four mani-pedis and four facials. Is that right?" Mom nodded.

"Fantastic. Come on back and follow me. I'll get you all set up." She stood from her desk and held her hand out. "I'm Amanda, by the way." My mom shook her hand and the girls and I smiled at her. She led us down a short hallway and up a couple of steps. Two pedicure chairs sat in a large room with light lavender walls and several vases of beautiful white orchids.

"We only have the two pedicure chairs, so we'll have to do you in two different groups. Is that okay?" Amanda asked as she stepped back, letting us pass.

Mom looked around. In the opposite corner of the room were two fancy white armchairs for us to sit in while we watched the girls get their first pedicures. "No problem." She smiled at Amanda.

Once Amanda was out of the room, the girls bounced around, inspecting everything. "Look at this flower, Lucy. There are crystals at the bottom." Piper stared wide-eyed at a vase with an orchid in it on the table.

"Mom, are these crystals?" Lucy asked.

"Kinda. They're really shiny beads," I answered, twirling their ponytails in my fingers as I stood behind them.

Mom went over and set her purse down as the door opened and two more young girls came in. "Hi, I'm Rachel," said the exotic-looking girl with doe eyes, a nose ring, and *really* curly hair. "And this is Audra." Audra was a little more ordinary looking with a cute bob and rosy cheeks.

"Good morning," Audra greeted us with a wave.

Rachel clapped her hands together and scoped the four of us out. "Who's going first?"

"Me! Me!" Lucy and Piper made me laugh with the way they were hopping up and down like puppies in a pet store.

"I guess they wanna go first." I giggled. "I'm assuming it's okay if we sit over here?"

"Of course. Make yourselves comfortable." Rachel walked over and took the lilac and sage-green pillows off the chairs and set them on the white dresser. "Have a seat. Can we get you a drink?"

"Uh . . . I'm driving. I'll just have some hot tea, please," Mom answered.

"Oooo, I'll take a mimosa." I grinned.

"Mom, can I have a . . . mimmermosa too?" Piper asked.

I chuckled at her version of the word. "Sorry, babe. Not for a few more years, but how about some orange juice? It looks just like a mimosa."

Lucy and Piper both nodded and Rachel disappeared out the door.

The morning was flying by too quickly.

"Are they the cutest things you've ever seen in your whole life or what?" Mom said, blowing on her hot tea as we watched Lucy and Piper getting their feet pampered. They sat in the big chairs, looking tinier than ever, holding their champagne flutes full of orange juice as Rachel and Audra massaged their little feet and polished every little toenail.

"They *are* the cutest. I'm pretty crazy about them." I couldn't help but grin at my sweet daughters.

"I'm pretty crazy about *you*," my mom said, leaning in close.

My head snapped to meet her glassy eyes and trembling chin. Instinctively, I reached out and put my hand on hers. "What's this about?"

She shrugged and plucked a tissue from her purse, dabbing at her eyes. "I don't know. My only baby is getting married soon and I'm emotional. I'm also so damn proud of you, Kacie. I can't believe all you've accomplished on your own since you had them."

"I wasn't exactly on my own." I squeezed her hand gently. "You've been there for me since the day I found out I was pregnant, Mom. Way before Zach even left. I couldn't have done *any* of this without you."

"I'm glad you feel that way, Kacie, but you totally could have. You're the strongest woman I know." She sniffed.

"It takes a strong woman to raise a strong woman."

"Oh God, look at me." She laughed awkwardly as she wiped her eyes again. "If I'm like this now, how can I possibly get through your actual wedding?"

Giggling, I nodded my head toward Lucy and Piper. "Just focus on them instead. They're usually good for a few laughs."

We left the spa a couple of hours later with smooth skin and pretty fingers and toes.

"Do you have to get back, or do you have time for a late lunch?" Mom asked.

"Um . . ." I glanced at my phone. "Sure. Alexa and I were supposed to go over some last-minute flower details, but I can't get her to text me back."

"There's a really nice Italian restaurant that just opened down the street here. Wanna check it out?"

It wasn't worth driving, so we walked the two little blocks to Cellucci's. The hostess welcomed us, grabbed a few menus, and asked us to follow her. We walked past a handful of empty tables and I wondered why we were being led all the way to the back of the restaurant. We passed through a set of large, wooden saloon doors and—

"Surprise!"

My head whipped forward and my mouth fell open.

Alexa, Lauren, Darla, Shae, and JoAnn all stood near a large table in the middle of the room, which was exploding with flowers and balloons and streamers. Mom and the girls turned to face me, and once again, tears filled my mom's eyes.

"What's going on?" My hands covered my mouth as my eyes darted around the whole room.

Lauren walked up and pulled me into a tight hug. "A surprise shower, silly."

"But I said—"

"We know, we know. You didn't want a shower." Mom rolled her eyes. "But your friends are excited and wanted to celebrate with you. Me too, so have fun."

Max wobbled over, wrapping his chubby arms around Lauren's leg. I bent down and gathered him up. "Hey, buddy."

Darla came over and hooked her arm through Lauren's. "Blondie here says this place has great food."

Lauren laughed, glancing at Darla and back at me. "Why haven't I met her before? She's hilarious."

JoAnn walked up with Shae and planted a kiss on my cheek. "Congrats, honey. I know you and Brody aren't technically married yet, but I already think of you as a daughter."

Before I could get a word in to respond, Shae threw her arms around me, squishing Max and me together. "Congratulations. I'm so happy for you guys."

I tried shifting Max to my other hip as I hugged her back. "Thanks for driving all this way. I can't believe you guys did all this."

"That Alexa, she's quite the party planner, huh?" My mom gave JoAnn a quick hug.

Craning my neck to the left, I peeked at Alexa, who was standing next to the table, rocking Joseph in her arms. I passed Max back to Lauren. "I'll be back in a minute, okay?" Lauren and Darla nodded.

"Hey." I hip-bumped Alexa.

"Hey. Congratulations." She smiled at me.

"Thanks for this. For everything."

"Nah, don't mention it. It's the least I could do for the girl who's been my best friend for years and years."

Resting my hip against the edge of the table, I looked out at my best friends and family, all gathered in the room to celebrate my wedding to Brody, and laid my head on Alexa's shoulder. "How do you always know? I said I didn't want a shower, yet you knew I'd love it."

Her shoulder raised, then lowered with a hefty sigh. "When are you gonna learn, Kacie? Alexa is always right." She smiled.

12

BRODY

Tomorrow I'm marrying the girl of my dreams. I take that back. I'm marrying the girl of every man's dreams. I'm just the lucky bastard that tricked her into picking him. I hear my friends joke a lot about getting married and having an ol' ball and chain, but to be honest, I was so excited to marry Kacie that I wasn't kidding when I offered to fly her out to Vegas and elope the night I proposed. I'm glad we waited, though.

The barn looked amazing, I had a special tux made for Diesel to be the ring dog, and I was beyond ready for some Oreo wedding cake. The one thing I couldn't wait for was to watch Kacie walk down the aisle toward me, hold my hand, and swear to love me for the rest of her life. Everything else would forever pale in comparison to that moment.

Kacie and I had agreed not to see each other for a few days before the wedding, but I had something to give her and I couldn't wait anymore. I knocked on the big wooden door of the inn and took a few steps back. The knob turned and four tiny fingers curled around the front of the door. As it pulled back farther, Lucy saw me, and her big brown eyes widened in response.

"Brody!" She flung the door all the way open and jumped into my arms.

"Hey, kiddo." I kissed the side of her head. "Where is everyone?"

"Brody!" Piper came flying out of the house and leaped into my free arm.

"They're in the family room. Come in." Lucy giggled, covering her mouth.

I was walking through the hall toward the kitchen area with one Twinkie in each arm when Sophia spotted us. She did a quick double take and held her hands up, halting me in my tracks. "Stop!" she yelled. "She's trying on her dress."

"What? Brody's here?" Kacie hollered. "We aren't supposed to see each other till tomorrow."

"Sorry." I shrugged. "I couldn't wait."

As I stood in the hallway making goofy faces at the girls, Sophia watched Kacie take her dress off but kept a close eye on me to make sure I didn't try to sneak a peek.

Smart lady.

"Okay." Sophia waved us into the room. "She's gone."

I laughed as we made our way into the kitchen, where I deposited the girls at the island. "Sorry about that. What are the odds that the exact moment I stop by, she's trying on her dress?"

Sophia shook her head back and forth. "That was close."

"Tell me about it. I saw my life flash before my eyes." I winked at her. "So what's everyone up to?"

"What are you doing here?" Kacie came down the hall from their apartment quickly. "Is everything okay?"

"Everything is fine." I caught her as she barreled into my chest. I felt bad that I'd worried her. "I actually just wanted to steal you and the Twinkies for a couple minutes. Is that okay?"

"Sure . . ." She sounded perplexed.

This oughta really throw her for a loop, then.

"And"—I took three blindfolds out of my back pocket—"would you please wear these?"

Blinking a couple of times in confusion, Kacie furrowed her brows and looked to her mom for answers. Sophia chuckled and shrugged her shoulders as she wiped down the kitchen table. "Don't ask me. I quit trying to figure this boy and his tricks out months ago."

The girls skipped over and happily took the blindfolds, with their hesitant mom right behind them.

"We have to wear these now?" Kacie asked.

"Yep," I answered.

She sighed and shook her head. "I have no idea what this means."

I'd never forget how cute my three girls looked, standing in the kitchen completely confused, wearing dark purple blindfolds.

"Okay. Lucy and Piper, hold hands, then Lucy, hold your mom's hand," I ordered.

They did as I asked and I took a tight hold of Piper's hand. "Okay, I'm leading the way with Piper. We're going to walk nice and slow."

"If I fall and have a black eye for the wedding, you're dead meat," Kacie warned playfully. The girls giggled hard at their mom's threat.

I led them out the front door, onto the porch. "We're going down four steps in a second. Be careful."

Lucy and Piper counted as we walked. "One, two, three, four."

"Good job, guys. Keep going." I held Piper's little hand as we walked slowly, one foot in front of the other, about one hundred yards into the woods. I kept peeking back to make sure everyone was upright and no one was crashing into any trees. We came to a clearing and my heart started racing. I was beyond nervous for them to see what I'd done.

"All right, here we are. Kacie, take your blindfold off first."

Her hand slid the blindfold up her forehead just a tad before she saw what I'd led them to and gasped. With her mouth hanging open and her eyes wider than I'd ever seen them, I whispered to her, "Watch their faces."

"Okay, Twinkies, take off your blindfolds."

They lifted their hands to their blindfolds and ripped them off, squinting against the sun until they saw it.

Their castle.

Technically it was a playhouse, but it was the mother of all playhouses. Piper screamed so loud I'm pretty sure she sent animals within a five-mile radius running for their lives, while Lucy stood frozen, just like her mother, not able to form a response.

"What do you guys think?" I laughed.

"Can we go in it?" Piper started running toward it before I could answer her, with Lucy trailing right behind.

"I . . . what did you . . . this is . . ." Kacie stuttered, shaking her head slowly.

"Told you I'd get them a castle." I nuzzled her neck. "Come on. You have to see this thing." Grabbing her hand, I pulled her toward it. Admittedly, I was as excited as the girls were, maybe more.

As we ducked our heads under the arched front door of Lucy and Piper's new castle, Kacie's eyes skimmed the whole room. The girls ran from the first floor up the wooden spiral staircase to the second.

"It has a staircase?" Kacie's voice squeaked.

"Hell yeah, it has a whole second story on it. And look at this." I reached past her and flicked a light switch next to the front door, making the overhead light flip on. "Working electrical." I wiggled my eyebrows at her.

"This is insane. It's even painted like a real castle. Who did that? Is this drywall or brick?" She slid her hand along the smooth wall. "And is that a sink?" Rambling off question after question, she spun in circles, trying to take it all in.

I laughed, attempting to keep up as she wandered around the first floor. "Yes, it's drywall, but I had an artist come in and paint it to look like real stone. And yes, that's a sink that will eventually have running water."

Kacie turned to face me, still completely baffled. "Brody, this is amazing, but it's too much."

"It's not even close." I walked over and put my hands on her shoulders, bending my knees until I was eye to eye with her. "I promised my Twinkies a castle. No way was I letting them down."

She sighed happily and slid her arms around my waist, resting her head against my chest.

"I'm not done."

Her head snapped back. "What?"

"I have one more surprise."

"Brody, I don't think they can handle any more today."

"This one isn't for them." I walked over to the little kitchen counter and picked up a small box about the size of a phone book. "This one's for you. It's your wedding present."

"First of all, our wedding is tomorrow. Secondly, I don't know if I can take any more today either." She bit her lip and looked up at me.

"Open it."

She slid the ribbon off and removed the lid, revealing a piece of paper. Her face twisted in confusion as she tried to control her eyes enough to read it. "What is this?"

"I know we agreed we weren't gonna talk about where to live until after the wedding, and I hope you're not mad, but I made a decision. That's a property deed to the land we're standing on. I bought it from your mom." I grinned even though she wasn't looking at me. "Lift the paper."

Her hand moved the sheet off to the side, exposing the cover to a huge book of house plans.

"Pick one."

Her hand flew to her throat as she took a stumbling step back, looking at me incredulously. "Are you serious?"

"I'm serious, Kacie. Let's live here, next to your mom and Fred and the lake and our pier. I *want* to live here. I want the girls to grow up here, just like you did. I want all of our kids to grow up here."

"But your condo, you love that condo." Her hands were shaking as she rubbed the sides of her face, still not fully comprehending what she was hearing.

"I do love that condo, so I was thinking, why don't we keep that condo in case you and the girls come to a late game and we don't want to drive all the way back here after? The commute isn't that bad for me, and it's really only three-quarters of the year I have to make the drive anyway." The girls stomped through the second floor above our heads as I took Kacie's hands in mine. "Come on, what do ya say? Let's build here."

A heavy sigh shuddered through Kacie's body as she closed her eyes, opening them when she exhaled. "I'm still waiting to wake up from this dream, where I find out you aren't real, that none of this is real."

"You're awake, babe. We both are and we're gonna live out these dreams together."

She rolled her tongue in between her teeth and her lip. "All right, Murphy. Let's do it. Let's build a house."

"Yes!" I fist-pumped in the air. "I built a castle for my princesses, now it's time to build one for my queen!"

I reached around Kacie's waist and pulled her toward me, closing the space between us and tilting her face up. She lifted onto her tippy-toes and pressed her lips against mine. She tasted sweet, like strawberries. I eased her lips apart gently with mine and swiped my tongue against hers. Her hands fisted the cotton of my T-shirt and she dragged me tighter against her.

Lucy and Piper came flying down the stairs, causing us to break our kiss and settle for a hug. "Mom, you have to come look at this! There are beds up here."

"And a bathroom!"

Kacie narrowed her eyes at me and cocked her hip to the side, crossing her arms over her chest. "A bathroom?"

"What if they have to pee?" I grinned, grabbing Kacie's hand and pulling her upstairs.

13

KACIE

I'd learned that every bride worries about the little things that could potentially go wrong during her wedding. Maybe the flower girl pouts and refuses to walk down the aisle, maybe someone has a coughing fit during the vows, maybe a groomsman drinks too much and passes out in a corner. Those were the types of horror stories I'd been hearing from every person I came across over the last couple of months, all the way down to the cashier at the grocery store telling me that her now-husband cried during his vows and it pissed her off. It pissed me off too, frankly. Not that he cried during his vows, but that she was mad about it. When did the world become so worried about the wedding and less excited about the *reason* for that wedding?

That's what I was excited for, to spend the rest of my life with Brody. Our wedding was just a party to celebrate that first day, in my eyes. I didn't care if the cake tipped over or if my dress ripped, as long as I was Mrs. Brody Murphy at the end of it all.

"Mommy?" Piper's little voice pulled me off my wedding soapbox and back to reality.

"I'm awake, baby. Come on in." I sat up in bed and glanced at the clock on my nightstand.

Seven forty-five.

Piper's crazy morning hair shot out in ten different directions as she slowly made her way across my bedroom. I pulled the covers back as she climbed up next to me, tucking us back in tight. I hooked my right arm around her and laid my head on hers. "What's going on?"

"I'm nervous."

"Nervous? How come?"

"What if I don't do good today?" Her voice trailed off.

"What do you mean?" I shifted to the side so that I could look her in the eye.

She shrugged. "Lucy told me yesterday that I walk too fast and throw too many flowers. I tried telling her it was just practice and I'd do better during the real wedding, but I'm scared. What if I mess up again?"

"Oh, honey." I hooked my arms around her and pulled her into my lap. "First of all, there's no rule as to how many flowers you can drop at once, nor is there a rule about walking slow. You just do whatever feels right for you, and Lucy will have to deal with it. I know you're gonna do an amazing job, and I can't wait to walk down the aisle and see you."

Her shoulders relaxed as she leaned into me. "Okay."

We didn't say anything else. We just sat snuggled up in my bed, rocking back and forth as she thought about conserving her flowers and walking slow. All I could think about was how lucky I was to be her mom.

If you would've told me a year ago that I'd be getting my hair done for my wedding while sitting in Brody's mom's kitchen, I would've told you you were crazy. Yet there I sat on a wooden kitchen chair with my stylist, Sammie, putting huge, heavy curlers in my hair.

"Are you nervous?" Alexa asked.

I shrugged. "Not really. I'm just ready to see him and get this started."

Lauren and my mom sat in two other chairs, with two of Sammie's assistants standing behind them.

"You have the most beautiful hair." One of them gawked at Lauren's long blond layers.

"Ugh," groaned Alexa, dropping her cereal bowl into the sink. "Would you believe she wakes up like that? It's disgusting."

"She does." I laughed. "Luckiest girl in the world."

"Honey, I'm gonna take your dress up to Brody's room, okay?" JoAnn appeared in the doorway carrying my wedding dress bag.

"Sure, thanks." I smiled.

"Wait, Brody built this house for his parents, right?" Alexa rubbed her chin, staring off into space as she tried to remember.

"Yep."

"Then why does he have a bedroom here?"

"It's not like a childhood bedroom. You'll see when we go up there. It's actually pretty cool."

An hour or so later, we all looked absolutely stunning from the neck up. From the neck down, we all had on baggy button-down plaid shirts. Lucy's and Piper's went all the way to their ankles, which they thought was hilarious.

"Okay." I took a deep breath. "Dress time."

We all walked slowly upstairs, careful not to lose a bobby pin or uncurl a curl. I opened the door to Brody's room and everyone filed inside.

"Holy crap." Alexa spun slowly with her mouth open. "It's like a Brody shrine."

She was right. The room did have a big bed and a large couch in it, in case Brody ever wanted to spend the night, but it was so much more than that. A large, dark walnut shelf sat prominently in the middle of the largest wall, and it was overflowing with Brody's hockey memorabilia, both from the Wild and from college. His college goalie helmet sat on the top shelf with a tiny spotlight on it. Dozens of glossy action shots and newspaper articles were framed and stuck in between hockey pucks and sets of gloves, each with its own significance. I stared at the big shelf, feeling a little sad that I hadn't known him then. I know if I had, things between us might not be the same, but I wish I could've seen him get his first NHL save.

"Awww!" Lauren's coos pulled me from my trance. I turned toward the door as Lucy and Piper walked into the room in their ice-blue dresses, with my mom following along behind. My hands flew up to my mouth and tears stung my eyes when I saw them. They looked so grown-up with their blond hair pulled up in loose buns and a few soft pieces curling around their faces.

I walked over to them and squatted when I got close. "You guys look *so* beautiful. No one's gonna notice me today, because they're going to be too busy looking at you." I sniffed.

Neither responded, but they both smiled shyly, not used to all the attention.

"Is that mascara?" I squinted and got closer to Lucy.

"Uh-huh. Gigi put it on us." She beamed.

Mom winked at me. "Just a tad."

"You two are just the sweetest little things," JoAnn said, shaking her head slowly. "Kacie, I'm gonna leave you girls to get dressed. I have to get ready myself."

"I'm gonna take them and head downstairs too." My mom followed. "You three need to get moving and you don't need us gawking at ya. We'll see you downstairs in a bit."

I bent down and planted soft kisses on Lucy's and Piper's cheeks. "See you soon, loves."

"Kacie, what's this?" Lauren picked up a small blue box on the desk. "It has your name on it."

"It does?" I took a couple of steps across the room and she handed it to me.

It was a simple little ice-blue box with a perfectly wrapped white ribbon on it. Before I lifted the lid, I knew exactly who it was from, though that didn't lessen my shock when I saw the shiny necklace looking back at me. It was a beautiful, delicate white gold chain with a large diamond in the middle and two stones, one on either side.

"Wow, that's so gorgeous." Lauren peered over the top of the box.

"It really is," Alexa agreed. "Are those emeralds?"

"No." I shook my head as a small smile crossed my lips. "They're peridot, the birthstone for August."

"Oh my God . . ." Alexa took a step back, tilting her head to the side as she laughed incredulously. "Lucy's and Piper's birthstone."

I nodded at her as a tear rolled down my cheek.

"No. No. No crying," Lauren squeaked as she jumped up and grabbed a tissue off the desk. "Your makeup looks fantastic. No more crying."

"Sorry." I sniffled as she wiped my eyes.

Alexa took the box from me and set it back on the desk. "Hurry up. Get in your dress so I can put that thing around your neck."

Lauren unzipped the bag and pulled my dress out as Alexa helped me undo my buttons. "Do you think he knew, about the birthstones?"

"He knew." I nodded confidently. "He pays attention like that."

"Wait." Alexa stood up and stared me square in the eye, pulling her perfect brows in tight. "Did you get him a wedding present?"

My face grew hot as I looked toward the ground, not wanting my friends to see me blush.

Alexa gasped. "What did you do?"

"Nothing," I snapped defensively. "I'm not telling you guys. It's embarrassing."

"Like hell you aren't." Lauren was practically drooling as she abandoned my wedding dress and sat on the edge of the couch. "Spill it, girl."

Sighing, I peeked around the corner to make sure Brody's mom wasn't coming down the hallway. I closed the door quietly and plopped down on the bed, dropping my head into my hands. After another deep breath, I looked at Alexa and Lauren, pleading with my eyes. "You guys can't tell *anyone*, promise?"

They nodded in unison, both of them leaning forward slightly.

"Okay, here goes. You know how sometimes women get those photo shoots done in like, lingerie and stuff for their boyfriends or husbands?"

Lauren sat up straight, clapping her hands like a teenager. "Oh my God, yes! Like a boudoir photo shoot?"

The back of my neck heated as I nodded. "Well, I did that. Some in lingerie and some in . . . hockey stuff, like his jersey and helmet. Stuff like that."

"Holy shit, you're the coolest wife ever! I got Derek a flask for our wedding. He was so excited I thought he was gonna hump it." Alexa rolled her eyes.

"You *are* the coolest ever." Lauren's sparkling eyes were wide as could be. "I'm not brave enough to do something like that. Good for you."

I shrugged. "I just wanted to step out of the box. You know how shy I can be when it comes to certain things. I wanted to shock him a little."

Lauren stood and picked up my wedding dress again, carrying it over to me. "Put this on. We gotta move. Did you give them to him yet?"

"I was too chicken," I admitted, glancing back and forth between the two of them, "so I left the album in a pretty box in the workshop, where the boys are hanging out right now, with a note that read 'Open when you're alone.'"

"Oh, great. So if he's hard when we walk into the barn, we'll know why," Alexa joked.

"Deep breath. You ready, kiddo?" Fred squeezed my hand as we stood by the side of the barn all alone, waiting for the bridesmaids to finish walking in. I would've given anything to see Lucy and Piper walk down the aisle, tossing their flowers as they grinned at all the attention, all while leading Diesel down with them, our rings tied around his neck. Thank God for videographers. When Brody told me he wanted Diesel in the wedding, I laughed at first. I thought he was kidding. He looked offended, whining that my babies were in the wedding; he wanted his baby to be too. So we went out and bought an ice-blue leash and collar to match the tux Brody'd had made for him.

"I'm so ready. I can't wait to see him. Them. Everyone." My stomach twisted and churned as I listened intently for the barn doors to close. That was our cue to move to the front and wait for them to open back up.

"Did you guys decide what you were doing with your vows? Your mom mentioned you were talking about it the other day," he asked, trying to keep me calm and distracted.

"We decided to go with traditional vows. Actually, *I* decided. I can't help it. There's something romantic about reciting the same promise that people have been saying for decades and decades."

"I think that's sweet."

I reached out and straightened the collar of Fred's tux. "I think *you're* sweet, Fred. You look so handsome."

He lifted his hand and gently rubbed my cheek with the backs of his fingers. "No one's gonna be looking at me, baby girl."

"Stop it." I lifted my eyes toward the sky as I waved at them to keep them dry. "No crying before the wedding. It's a rule."

Fred laughed as we heard the doors close. "Here we go." He smiled.

He offered his arm to me, which I gladly accepted. My heart started beating faster with each step we took toward the barn entrance, and suddenly I was worried that I was going to pass out. The barn doors would open and people would turn to watch the bride walk, but instead they'd see me lying in a heap on the ground with Fred standing over me, not sure what the hell to do.

Maybe we should have just eloped.

Seconds before a full-blown panic attack took over my whole body, the rusty hinges of the barn door squeaked, and Big Mike's face smiled at me as he pushed one of the barn doors open. Shea's new husband, Ricky, opened the other one.

"Looking good, Sis." He grinned as he shifted the door all the way open and stood behind it.

The minute the doors opened, a weird calm washed over me, taking my jittery nerves right along with it. I glanced over the sea of fifty or so of our family and best friends and immediately looked for Brody.

I needed to find him.

I needed to see him, but the sun was in my eyes.

The band started playing "Here Comes the Bride" softly, and we started walking. Two steps into the barn and the sun shifted, allowing me a clear view of the front of the barn.

There he stood. My man. Looking sharper than I'd ever seen him in his black tuxedo with a black vest underneath, slightly different from his groomsmen, who wore ice-blue vests under their jackets. Brody stood tall, calm and cool as ever, until we locked eyes. That's when the mood shifted from light to intense. I bit my lip hard, determined to keep it together and not cry the whole way down the aisle. I recalled Fred saying something to me, but I couldn't for the life of me remember what it was. All I could focus on was Brody.

When we finally, after what felt like twenty minutes, reached the front of the barn, I was desperate to touch Brody but needed to wait my turn. Fred turned and gave me a slow kiss on the cheek, lingering for just a second before he turned to Brody. Fred offered his hand, but Brody grabbed his shoulders and pulled him in for a bear hug as our guests chuckled. They pulled apart, and Fred joined my mom in the front row, squeezing her hand as he sat down. I stepped toward Brody and reached for his hands.

"You look beautiful," he leaned in and whispered as the band finished playing.

I reached up and touched my new necklace, mouthing "thank you" back to him.

He cocked an eyebrow at me, and the sexiest smirk tugged at the left side of his lips as he leaned in one more time. "Thank *you*."

My face flushed instantly as I realized he was talking about the pictures.

The music stopped playing and our ceremony began.

A small speech from the officiant.

Candle lighting.

Then came time for our vows, and I was hell-bent on not crying my way through them.

Brody went first. He took my hands and stared straight at me with his stunning green eyes. "I, Brody Michael, take you, Kassandra Elizabeth, to be my wife, to have and to hold, from this day forward, for better or for worse, for richer, for poorer, in sickness and in health, to love and to cherish, until death do us part."

Brody nailed it, like he'd been practicing for weeks. He made it look easy.

Our officiant turned toward me, signaling me to start.

My hands shook as I took a deep, cleansing breath. "I, Kassandra Elizabeth, take you, Brody Michael, to be my husband, to have and to hold from this day forward, for better or for worse, for richer, for poorer, in sickness and in health, to love and to cherish, until death do us part." My voice started cracking as I rushed the last part out.

Brody's eyes never left mine. In that moment, I felt like we were the only two people in that whole barn, maybe even the whole world. I meant every letter of every word of every sentence in my vows. No matter what came our way, we would conquer it, together.

Time for the rings.

The officiant took a deep breath. "Here's where we would normally do the ring ceremony"—my head snapped over to him—"and I promise it's coming. But first there is one more set of vows to be said."

Before I had time to be confused about what was going on, Brody released me and took a step to his left, out toward our guests. Lucy and Piper walked up to him and each took one of his hands as he squatted down. Out of the corner of my eye, I saw my mom's hand fly up to her mouth, and the guests let out a collective, "Awww," as I tried to breathe past the huge lump in my throat.

Piper peeked up at me and grinned before looking back at Brody.

"Okay, you guys ready? Just like we practiced, okay?" he whispered.

"I, Brody, promise to love you, Lucy and Piper, just as much as I love your mommy. I promise to love you and protect you and always take care of you, no matter what. From this day forward, you will always and forever be my Twinkies. And I Twinkie swear to always kill all the spiders." He held up his pinkie fingers and the girls giggled as they wrapped theirs around his.

Every woman in the barn wiped her eyes as Alexa bumped my elbow to get my attention. I turned to my side and she handed me a wad of tissues. Holy crap, did I need them.

Lucy lifted her hand to Piper's ear and whispered something to her. They recited in unison, "We love you, Brody, and we're happy you're marrying our mommy. Thank you for our castle." The room erupted in light laughter as Brody's head fell toward the floor, bouncing with his own laughter. He peeked up at me and grinned. "They wrote their vows all by themselves."

Brody stood up and turned, taking something from Andy. When he turned back around, he walked behind the girls and placed a necklace, identical to the one he'd given me, around each of their necks before squatting back down and pulling them into a loving hug.

I tried my best to contain my sobs but was losing the battle a little more every second. I'd had no idea they were going to do that. It was the most amazing surprise ever.

The girls walked back behind me and took their places with Lauren and Alexa as Brody stood before me and took my hands one more time. I couldn't believe I was expected to carry on with the rest of the ceremony after that. All I wanted to do was wrap my arms around the man standing in front of me and never let go.

Never. Ever. Let. Go.

Brody placed my ring on my finger and I placed his ring on his.

The officiant closed his book and a big grin crossed his face. "I hereby pronounce you husband and wife, you may now . . . pay the toll."

Once again, my eyes flicked to him and then immediately back to Brody, who smirked and winked at me before closing in and softly placing his lips on mine. He slid one hand around my waist while gently gripping the back of my head with the other one and pulled me in tight against him. Our guests cheered and hollered.

It was our first kiss as husband and wife, but easily the most intimate one we'd ever shared.

14

BRODY

After the ceremony, everyone had to exit the barn so the staff could move the chairs and set up the tables. I took that opportunity and grabbed Kacie's hand to steal her away for a few minutes.

I closed the door to my dad's workshop and pulled the curtain before turning around and grabbing Kacie's face, planting a firm kiss right on her lips. She opened her mouth, inviting me in, and my tongue RSVP'd happily. We stood for a few minutes kissing, hugging, and rocking back and forth.

"We did it." I was breathless when she finally pulled back. "We're married."

"I know." Her eyes sparkled as she rewarded me with the biggest smile I'd ever seen on her face. Her pink lips were swollen from my kiss, but I didn't care. It was our wedding, we were in love, and we could do what we wanted as much as we wanted. "Seriously, did someone challenge you to see how many times you could surprise me today, or what?"

"No, but I'd gladly take that challenge." I laughed, kissing her again.

"I was emotional enough with the necklace this morning, but then the vows with Lucy and Piper and the necklaces for them?" She shook her head slowly back and forth. "I don't even know what to say, Brody. You've made this whole day so special."

I hooked my finger under her chin and raised her face to mine. "It's the least I could do. You've made my *life* special."

Her eyes filled with tears again, and she pulled a tissue out of her cleavage.

"Got anything else in there?" I joked, yanking the front of her dress out just a bit and peeking down it.

A huge smile broke out across her face as she dried her eyes. "I'm thinking you saw what was down my dress earlier with that photo album."

"What photo album?" I asked.

Her face fell serious. "The black album? I left it here for you earlier, with a note on it?"

I shook my head back and forth. "I didn't see an album."

All blood drained from her face as her eyes bulged.

"Kacie, Kacie, I'm just kidding. Relax." I grabbed on to her shoulders and held tight, just in case she passed out. "Babe?"

"You ass!" She punched my chest as hard as she could with her tiny fist. "You nearly gave me a heart attack! A heart attack on my wedding day, of all days."

"I'm sorry." I laughed, not really feeling all that sorry. "I just wanted to freak you out."

"Mission accomplished." She narrowed her eyes and glared playfully at me.

"You deserved it."

"For what?" Her tone raised defensively.

"That album. It was the hottest thing I've ever seen in my twenty-eight years on this planet. I sat here and looked at it for about ten minutes, and my dad came in and wanted to have a heart-to-heart talk before the other guys got here. I had to hide behind his workbench for another ten minutes before my hard-on went away."

Kacie threw her head back and laughed hard, exposing her sexy neck.

I took advantage of the opportunity, kissing, biting, and sucking on her. "You're evil," I groaned in between kisses.

"Mmmm, I'm glad you liked them," she moaned, "but that was only half your present. I'll give you the other half later tonight when we're alone."

I nipped at her clavicle area, tasting her sweet skin. "I like the sound of that."

"No, you hornball." She giggled. "I really have something for you, but I wanted to see your face when you opened it."

A knock at the door brought us back to reality. Kacie walked over and opened it as I hid behind the workbench again. Barely through the door, Viper swept Kacie up in his arms and spun her around as she squealed.

"Congratulations, Mrs. Murphy."

"Thanks, Viper." She reached up and planted a small kiss on his cheek. "Who knew you'd clean up this nicely? You cut your hair and everything."

"I know." He ran his fingers through his newly trimmed blond hair. "I don't remember the last time it was this short. Seems to be working, though. I got two hot nurses' phone numbers already." He flashed an evil grin before turning to head out the door. "Oh, by the way, they're all set up in there. Time to party!"

"Ready?" Kacie held her hand out for me.

I glanced down at the tent that was still half-pitched in my pants and back up at her. "Two more minutes."

We spent the next hour all alone at our little table for four, gorging on lobster, rosemary chicken, baby red garlic mashed potatoes, and green beans that were so fresh they squeaked in between your teeth.

It was time for our first dance, and I was beyond ready for it. The band played an amazing cover of Sara Evans's song "I Could Not Ask for More" as Kacie and I swayed back and forth in each other's arms.

"I can't believe it's half over already." She sighed as she rested her head against my chest.

"It's gone by so fast."

"I know, but I can't wait to get back and give you your gift."

"Stop talking about my gift, or you're going to have to stand in front of me for a while."

Her laugh vibrated against my hand as it rested on her back. "I told you, it's not *that* kind of gift, though that can probably be arranged too."

Our song ended and I led Kacie to a chair near the end of the dance floor. Puzzled, she pulled her brows in tight and looked at me as I sat her down and kissed the top of her hand before walking away.

"Twinkies, would you please meet Brody out in the middle of the dance floor?" the lead singer bellowed into the microphone. My eyes scanned the barn quickly, not sure which direction they were going to come from. Off to my left, they appeared through the crowd from behind Kacie, walking out to the dance floor slowly, with shy smiles on their faces.

Once they got to me, just like at Lauren's wedding the year before, I motioned for them to each hop on one of my feet and hold on for dear life while the band played "Brown Eyed Girl." All eyes were on us, but my eyes were only on them. I felt so lucky that I was gonna be able to watch these two grow up and, hopefully, have a positive influence on who they'd eventually become. Kacie and Lauren sat next to each other, holding hands as I danced with my Twinkies.

Life was so fucking good.

We danced the night away for a few more hours, until one by one, the guests started to trickle out. It was exhausting trying to make sure I talked to and thanked everyone, but so much fun at the same time. In all honesty, I was glad everyone was leaving. I couldn't wait to be alone with my wife.

Kacie teared up as we hugged our parents and the girls good-bye before heading out to my condo in the city. We had contemplated driving into the city in the morning to catch our flight to Hawaii, but decided that the extra hour of sleep would be more beneficial in the morning, rather than at night.

"I love you guys, so much. Be good for Gigi, okay?" Kacie sniffled as she hugged Lucy and Piper for the tenth time.

"We will, Mom." Lucy shut her eyes, squeezing them tight as she hugged her mom back.

"Will you bring us some seashells?" Piper asked as she clapped her tiny hands together.

I'll bring you the whole damn ocean, kid.

"We'll definitely bring you some shells, baby. Maybe a few presents too." Kacie brushed a few wisps of Piper's blond hair from her forehead.

"Honey, you guys still have a couple hours in the car. You'd better get going," Sophia warned. "We'll be fine. Go ahead."

"Okay." Kacie stood up and sighed. She turned to her mom and wrapped her arms around her shoulders, sniffling again. "Thanks so much, Mom. For everything."

"You are more than welcome, baby. You guys go, have the best honeymoon ever, and we'll see you in a week." Sophia winked at me over Kacie's shoulder as she hugged her back. "Don't let her stress about the girls too much."

"I won't." I grinned, knowing that would be next to impossible.

"Congrats again," Fred said firmly, extending his hand to me.

Looking down at his hand and back up at him, I raised one eyebrow. "Fred, you're my father-in-law now. Hug me for Christ's sake." I grabbed his hand and pulled him toward me for a bear hug.

We pulled out of the driveway, and Kacie turned back for one more look out the back window. I reached over and put my hand on her thigh, squeezing gently. "I love you, Mrs. Murphy."

Her eyes slid to mine, a soft, sexy haze filling them. "I love you more, Mr. Murphy."

Kacie and I talked nonstop, recounting all of our favorite wedding moments for the rest of the ride to my condo. One of my favorites was the actual ride itself: being in my truck with her, alone, listening to her giggle about all the little things while she wore black yoga pants and a silver hoodie that said Mrs. Murphy #30 on the back. Her hair was pulled into a messy ponytail and her new necklace hung from her neck, sparkling against the passing headlights.

After I was done checking her out, I noticed the black box on her lap. "Is that another photo album?" I asked hopefully.

Her head whipped toward me. "Oh my God, where *is* that?" Panic filled her voice.

I laughed out loud at her terror-filled face. "It's in the back."

"Thank goodness." Her shoulders slumped in relief. "And no, it's not another album. It's the other half of your present." She bit her lip nervously, tapping her fingers against the box as she stared down at her lap.

"What's the matter?"

"I'm just nervous about this one." She looked out the window, avoiding eye contact with me.

"Don't sweat it. I'm sure I'll love it."

We pulled into my parking garage and slowly made our way upstairs. Our legs felt heavy, weighed down by all the dancing and fatigue.

"It's weird coming in here without D running toward the door." I sounded like a sad little kid without his dog.

"I know. He'll have fun at your mom's this week, though." She threw herself down on my—*our*—couch, her eyelids looking heavy.

"Okay. Gimme that present so we can go consummate our marriage." I wiggled my eyebrows up and down as I plopped down next to her on the couch.

"Wow. That was romantic," she teased dryly.

I reached for the black box on the coffee table, barely lifting it before she slammed her hand down on the top, ripping it back toward her. "I'm not ready."

"Yes, you are. Give it to me." I laughed, lunging for it.

She held it out in the other direction, forgetting that my arms were longer than hers. I leaped toward her and tried to snatch the box out of her hand, accidentally knocking it to the floor instead. "Look. Now you made me drop it," I joked as I walked around to pick up the piece of cloth that fell out of it. Kacie sat up straight on the couch, hugging her legs to her chest.

"What is this?" I twisted what looked like a Minnesota Wild jersey in my hand, trying to make sense of it as Kacie watched me like a hawk. I finally found the shoulders and held it out in front of me. It was in fact a Minnesota Wild jersey, the tiniest one I'd ever seen, with an even tinier #30 and MURPHY stitched onto the back.

Holy. Shit.

I lowered my hands and stared at Kacie as my heart started pounding like an engine roaring to a start, all pistons pumping.

"Is this what I think it is?"

She nodded as she covered her eyes with her hands, peeking out from in between her fingers.

"You're—" I froze, unable to form any more words.

She nodded again, still hiding from me.

"When did you find out? How long have you known?" I held the little jersey up again, wondering how the hell anything could fit into it.

"I just found out last week. You don't want to know what I had to pay to have that shipped so fast." She was looking down at her lap, playing nervously with her new wedding band. Her eyes swept back up to me and she took a deep breath. "Are you okay?"

"Okay?" I roared, adrenaline coursing through my veins as I fist-pumped the air. "I'm better than okay. I'm fucking fantastic!" I ran over to my window and raised it as high as I could, sticking my head out into the warm summer air. "I'm gonna be a dad!" I yelled at the top of my lungs. I was sure it would be in the morning papers that Brody Murphy lost his mind and was screaming out of high-rise windows, but I didn't care. Turning around, I dived at Kacie, knocking her onto her back. I wrapped my arms around her and squeezed as hard as I could. "Oh, shit. I'm sorry." I rested my hand on her belly. "Are you okay? I didn't hurt you, did I?"

"No." She laughed as a tear dripped from her eye.

"Why are you crying?" I shifted to my side and wiped the tear that was rolling down her temple.

"These are happy tears, Brody. I was worried you were going to be upset."

I shook my head fast, moving my hand on top of hers. "I'm surprised, sure . . . but elated. After how much I love being a dad to the girls, I couldn't wait to make a baby with you. This is the best wedding present ever." I bent down and kissed the tip of her nose, the same cute nose I prayed our baby would have. "How do you feel? Are you okay?"

"I've actually felt really good, except for one annoying side effect." She chewed on the side of her mouth, trying not to smile.

"What's that?"

"Well, I have a lot of hormones going through my body right now, and I've been very . . ." Her eyes searched the room as she looked for her wording. "Uh . . . needy."

"Needy like horny?" I rejoiced, unable to keep the grin off my face.

"Mmhmm." She nodded.

"I can totally help with that, like right now." I stood up, reaching for her hands.

"Where are we going?" She sat up and unzipped her hoodie.

"In the bedroom. I'm not making love to my wife for the first time on the couch in my living room like some drunk, horny frat boy."

She slipped her hoodie off her shoulders and dropped it on the couch as she took my hand, following me to the bedroom.

I closed the bedroom door behind us and she started giggling as she sat on the edge of the bed.

"What?" I looked around the room, trying to figure out what she was laughing at.

"You. You closed the door."

"Yeah?"

"The girls aren't here." She bit her lip seductively, turning me on with just her sexy eyes. She'd had a sexy glow to her all night. I thought it was from the wedding, but now I realized there might be more to it.

"That's right." I whipped the door back open dramatically as I reached up and pulled my T-shirt over my head. Stalking across the room, I crawled over her as she scooted backward up the bed.

Gently resting my body weight to the side of her, I slid the strap of her tank top off her shoulder, kissing her smooth skin. "How does this work?" I asked in between kisses.

"Um . . . we've done it before. Have you forgotten?" She giggled again.

"No, I mean . . . is there anything special I need to do, or not do? Like, I don't want to bump its head."

Kacie's belly bounced up and down as she laughed hard at me. "It doesn't have a head yet. It's about the size of a blueberry right now. And no, sex can't hurt me. It's actually good for me."

"By all means, I want you to be as healthy as possible," I teased as I slid the other strap of her tank top down, exposing her lacy white bra. Grabbing the hem of her tank top, I lifted it up and over her head in one swift motion while I took her bra off with my other hand.

My hand immediately went to her exposed breast, cupping and squeezing it as she closed her eyes.

"Does that feel good?" I asked, growing harder by the minute.

"Yeah." She breathed heavily, lying back on the bed. "They're very sensitive lately."

I raised an eyebrow at her and licked my lips. "Good to know." Lowering my mouth just above her nipple, I decided I wanted to have a little fun with my new wife, take my time with her newfound sensitivity.

My tongue swirled the tip of her nipple very softly, just barely touching it. She responded by arching her back, forcing herself against me harder. I pulled back and switched to the other nipple. Repeating the same soft movements with my tongue, teasing and licking all the way around it. Every time she pushed herself against my mouth, silently begging for more pressure, I backed off just out of her reach.

"You're driving me nuts," she moaned.

"I know." An evil grin flashed across my lips. "This is fun. You've never reacted like this before."

"We haven't had much sex since I've been pregnant. Between all the wedding planning and stuff going on, our love life has been . . . lacking."

"I'm about to make up for that right now." I clamped my mouth down on her nipple and started sucking, hard.

"Oh, God," she moaned, arching her back again, except this time I didn't pull back. I kept circling her nipple with my tongue, alternating pressure as I flicked her other nipple with my thumb. The harder I sucked, the louder she moaned, until eventually she started bucking her hips against my thigh.

"Are you—"

"I'm coming!" she called out, grabbing my hand and shoving it down her yoga pants, in between her legs. Her panties were completely soaked, as were her inner thighs. I moved my fingers slowly, circling her swollen clit as I pulled her nipple back into my mouth, sucking gently this time. I couldn't take my eyes off her. Watching her convulse and come against my hand before her clothes were even off was the single most erotic experience of my life—so far.

Her pussy stopped pulsing and she opened her eyes and grinned, taking a deep breath. "Wow. Who knew I could come from nipple play?"

"Jesus, Kacie. That was the hottest thing I've ever seen." I grinned, letting my eyes travel the length of her body.

"Yeah?" Her beautiful, full lips curved into a seductive smile as she lifted her hips off the bed, sliding her pants off. "Now I want you to *feel* it."

"You don't have to tell me twice." I stood up and shoved my jeans off, leaving them in a heap on the floor as I climbed back into bed with her. "It's been a couple weeks and I'm pretty fucking turned on after that little show. I don't know how long I'll make it tonight."

"Good." She wrapped her hand around my cock and started stroking me slowly. "Because I'm ready to go again already."

"You are?" My eyes grew wide and I had to talk myself out of coming right there in her hand.

Picture frame. Water bottle. Snowflake. Bicycle.

"Mmhmm," she moaned, pushing me back on the bed. "Besides, we have a whole week in Hawaii ahead of us to work on your stamina." The sheets were cold against my back, sending a chill through my body. It didn't last long, though, as Kacie threw one leg over my hips and hovered above me. She picked my cock up with her tiny warm hand and angled it just right. Then I watched myself disappear inside of her wet pussy.

She rested her hands on my chest and closed her eyes, slowly moving up and down while she got used to me being inside her.

"Are you okay?" I was concerned I was hurting her, with the pained look on her face.

"God, yes," she panted as she picked up speed. With every thrust, her tits bounced up and down. Watching her pleasure herself on me made it harder and harder for me to hold on, but I really wanted her to get off again. I gripped her hips and started pumping into her as she slammed down against me. My balls started to tighten and I knew I only had seconds left.

"Oh, Brody!" Kacie called out, stilling above me. I could feel her pussy clenching around my cock, and I knew she was coming again. I dug my fingers into her skin and moved into her as deep as I could, exploding right along with her. My body shuddered as I came harder than I could ever remember in my whole fucking life.

When I opened my eyes, she was still moving slowly on top of me, but she was sitting back with a smile on her face.

"Wow." My chest heaved as I tried to slow my breathing.

"Agreed." She grinned as she rolled off me and snuggled into my side. "I think I'm liking like this married thing."

"Uh . . . if that's how it's gonna be"—I exhaled loudly as I puffed out my cheeks—"we're renewing our vows every week."

EPILOGUE

KACIE

"Stop it! That tickles!" I giggled, pulling away from Brody.

"You *really* want me to stop?"

"No." I pouted dramatically, sticking out my bottom lip. "You're not done yet."

"Then stop moving so I can concentrate," he laughed.

I held as still as possible as his hand curved around the bottom of my foot, gripping it lightly as he dragged the nail polish brush across my toenail. The tip of his tongue popped out of his mouth just a bit as he frowned, focusing on not getting any hot-pink polish on the surrounding skin.

I scrunched my eyes shut and tensed my whole body, trying not to wiggle too much, but every time he moved his hand against my foot, I damn near jumped out of my skin.

"Ah!" Yelling out, I pulled my foot back again.

Brody glared at me playfully, his beautiful green eyes shaded by his not-really-angry brows as he exhaled through his nose like a bull. "Do I have to hold you down?"

I rubbed my very swollen pregnant belly. "Isn't that how we got into this predicament in the first place?"

"Psh, whatever." He rolled his eyes. "There was no holding you down for that. It was more like trying to cover your mouth as you were screaming, 'More, Brody! More,'" he teased in a high-pitched voice as he humped the air. "Now hold still and let me finish."

"That's what he said." I giggled.

Brody huffed as he finished up the last couple of toes, flashing me warning glances out of the corner of his eye.

"You ready to go up to bed?" he asked as he blew on my pinkie toe.

"Yeah, I think tonight is the night. I can feel it," I said confidently, rubbing my belly again.

"You've said that the last two nights, babe." He patted my butt as I turned out the family room light, and we headed upstairs to our room. We'd been in our brand-new house for less than a month and it still smelled like fresh wood and new carpet. I loved it. We had decided on a large, five-bedroom craftsman-style model with clean lines and a cozy, woodsy interior. Brody had been such a trooper about helping me decorate and get everything ready before the birth of Little Murphy, even when I was too tired to go to the stores myself. He was constantly texting me pictures of furniture and lamps, schlepping home items that I'd given the thumbs-up to. And now, we were down to the wire.

"No, I mean it, I've been very crampy today and my back is killing me." I eased into bed, trying to convince myself that this would be the last night with this tiny alien in my belly. "Plus, I went on an extra-long walk with the girls today, even though I almost froze my tush off, *and* I ate two bowls of Mom's chili at dinner."

"Two bowls of chili?" Brody teased. "Maybe I should sleep on the couch."

"Very funny. Get over here and snuggle me."

My due date was only one week away, but I was not-so-silently begging this baby to come out tonight while Brody was home. He'd be leaving in the morning for a three-day road trip with the Wild, and while I knew it was a possibility, I *really* didn't want to have our baby without him.

"You know"—he pulled the covers back and crawled in next to me, his arm muscles flexing with each movement—"I've heard that vigorous sex sometimes triggers labor."

"I'm a labor and delivery nurse. You think I don't know that?" I rolled my eyes at him. "Plus, you used that last night and nothing."

"Nothing?" Brody sounded dramatically pained by my answer. "You called God's name so many times last night that either you were enjoying yourself or you were having a massive prayer session while in bed with me."

I smacked his chest and rolled onto my left side, facing him, so I could breathe easier.

"If you change your mind, you let me know." He kissed the tip of my nose. "I love you, baby."

"I love you too." I sighed happily.

He lifted my T-shirt and kissed my belly. "And I love *you*, baby."

He had done that every night he'd been home, and I swear the baby knew when he was there, responding with lots of little kicks after Brody talked to him, or her. It would be nice to know what we were having, but karma came around and smacked me in the face for teasing Alexa about not finding out. Brody refused. He wanted it to be a surprise. I would never admit it, because everyone knew I liked to be prepared, but I was excited for the surprise too. My whole relationship with Brody had been surprise after surprise, right down to this pregnancy, so it just seemed fitting that the sex of the baby be a surprise too.

The next morning, Lucy, Piper, and I sadly kissed Brody good-bye, and I switched from begging Little Murphy to come out to begging it to stay in. Brody would be home in three days. I could keep my legs together until then.

The first two days were a breeze. Lucy and Piper went to school during the day and I lay on the couch over at my mom's, keeping her company while they finished their own construction. With the money from the land she'd sold to Brody, she'd slowly redone all of the guest rooms and completely gutted the bathrooms on the guest wing of the inn. Now, she was working on her and Fred's end. She'd knocked down a few walls and reconfigured the apartment, downsizing from three to two bedrooms by combining two of the rooms into a large master suite. She was elated that construction was almost done and she'd soon have her apartment back. She was keeping the smaller bedroom as a playroom/guest room for Lucy and Piper, and eventually Little Murphy, to come and play at Gigi's house.

The third day was a little tougher. Braxton Hicks contractions were kicking my butt, making everything sore. Mom took the girls to school for me while I once again parked on her couch.

Zach would be picking Lucy and Piper up from school and taking them to his house for the weekend, but he was on notification that if Little Murphy decided to come out, we wanted the girls to come to the hospital.

"How ya feeling?" Fred asked, bringing me a blueberry bagel with plain cream cheese—my favorite.

I sighed. "Like I have an eight-pound bowling ball trying to drop out of me every second."

"Wow." Fred shook the image from his head and disappeared back into the kitchen.

After scarfing my bagel down like I was in a race with somebody, I decided that maybe a shower would be a good idea. I carried my plate to the kitchen. "All right, Fred. I'm gonna head home and shower."

He turned around from the sink and pulled his brows in tight, peeking at me over his glasses. "Want me to walk you?"

"Nah, I'm okay." I turned to leave and felt a big sneeze coming. Leaning against the island, I crossed my legs at my ankles and squeezed tight, prepping for the sneeze in advance. "Ah-choo!"

"Bless you."

"Thanks." I started walking out of the kitchen and exactly what I didn't want to happen, happened. Pee started dripping down my leg like an upside-down fountain.

"Uh . . ." Fred froze as he walked around the corner to inspect the splat noise he was hearing on his kitchen floor.

Wait.

That was a *lot* of pee. I clenched my muscles together to make it stop, but it didn't work. Holy crap, that wasn't pee—my water just broke!

"Fred!" I panicked, my eyes flashing to his.

"Do you need help to the bathroom?" he stuttered, reaching for some paper towels.

"My water just broke!" I yelled, waving my hands around like a completely insane first-time mom, not the calm and cool nurse I was supposed to be.

Fred's face turned red as he rubbed the back of his neck, staring at the puddle underneath me. "Uhhh . . . I don't know what that means."

I rubbed my eyes with my hands, praying this was all a dream and that I'd wake up and be sleeping on the couch. "It means that my water just broke and the baby is coming today."

Fred started running in circles from the island to the kitchen table, back to the island, back to the table.

"Fred!" I didn't want to move and slip and hurt myself or the baby. "Grab the phone and call my mom."

He took his phone out of his pocket, but before he could dial, the front door opened.

"Soph!" Fred called out, still staring at the puddle on the floor like he was afraid it was going to get up and start running after him.

"What's all the yelling about—" Mom froze when she walked around the corner. "Did you pee?"

"No. My water broke."

She gasped. "Holy shit!"

My mom never swore. I wanted to laugh, but I was afraid the pressure on my belly would force poor Little Murphy to slide out and land in the puddle on the kitchen floor.

"Here's what we have to do: Mom, you grab a towel and lay it on the seat of your car. Then we're going to drive to my house and grab the bag in the closet by the front door, and you're gonna drive me to the hospital. Fred, I know he's practicing before his game, but can you try and get a hold of Brody?"

"Sure thing. Do we know where he is?" Fred asked.

I sighed. "Chicago." All I could do was pray that the stars would align and he'd be able to get back in time.

Everyone started moving all at once. Mom grabbed a wad of paper towels and cleaned up the floor so that I could walk to the front door safely. Fred helped me down the steps and into the car while Mom ignored my plan and instead sprinted along the trail through the woods to my house and grabbed the bag. She sprinted back, threw it in the car, and we were off.

"Well look at you." Dr. Newman grinned at me as she came into the room and grabbed a set of latex gloves out of the box on the wall.

"Hi." I sighed. Using my arms, I tried to adjust myself to sit up in the bed.

"Relax, relax." She touched my shoulder, stopping me from getting up. "What's wrong? I thought you were ready to get this baby out of you."

"I am, but Brody's out of town. We can't get a hold of him."

Mom, who was sitting in a chair next to my bed, reached out and squeezed my hand. "Fred has left a few messages and we're gonna keep trying."

"Relax back. I'm just gonna check you real quick."

Dr. Newman's hand slipped under the blanket on my lap. A quick pinch as she was pulling her glove off, frowning slightly.

"What?" I asked, panic swelling up in my chest.

"How long ago did you say your water broke?"

"Uh . . ." I looked at my mom, and then at the clock on the wall. "About six hours ago?"

"And you had your epidural three hours ago?"

I nodded.

"Okay, because you're at nine centimeters. This baby will probably be here in about an hour, maybe less. We're gonna start prepping the room."

My heart sank. "Okay."

My mom stood up and draped her arm over my shoulders, leaning her head against mine. "Oh, honey, I know you're sad, but I'll be here, and we'll keep trying to get a hold of him. Maybe he can come home earlier and at least be here tonight sometime."

Everything from that point on moved very quickly. They had the room prepped in no time, my legs in stirrups, and Dr. Newman was in her gown with her clear face guard on, sitting at the end of the bed.

Taylor, one of my coworkers and good friends, stood next to me, watching the monitor and holding my hand.

"All right, Kacie. As soon as you feel the next contraction, go ahead and start pushing."

Tears streamed down my face, but I felt no pain. I didn't want to push. I wanted to keep this baby in until Brody got here and could see it. I wanted him to hold my hand and kiss my forehead. I wanted him to be the first one to hold his baby.

My stomach tightened up as a contraction started. I squeezed my mom's and Taylor's hands and closed my eyes tight, pushing as hard as I could as Taylor counted down for me, "Five . . . four . . . three . . . two . . . one. Relax."

My head fell back against the bed and more tears fell.

Taylor gasped above me.

I looked up at her, but she was looking somewhere past me, over my shoulder. I followed her eyes and my breath caught too.

A sob escaped me as he whipped his coat off and threw it on the chair in the far corner of the room, still wearing his practice jersey.

"What are you—how did you—" I started to ask questions, but another contraction started. My mom stood up quickly, with tears streaming down her face, and moved out of the way, allowing Brody to have the seat next to me. "Here, take her hand. It won't be long now," she whispered as she kissed his cheek.

I squeezed his hand tight and pushed again.

"Five . . . four . . . three . . . two . . . one. Relax." Taylor sniffed.

My head fell back again and I gasped for air.

"You're doing so good, baby." Brody leaned over and kissed my temple but didn't remove his lips, instead resting them against my head as if he somehow knew that I needed physical contact with him.

"Good job, Kacie. The head is right here. I can see it. A head full of dark hair." Dr. Newman's eyes popped up over the blanket. "One more good push oughta get the head out."

"You got this, Kacie. One more good one," Brody whispered into my ear. "Come on. Let's meet our baby."

A contraction started and I bore down as hard as I could, digging my chin into my chest, using every cell in my body to try and get Little Murphy out.

"Here we go!" Dr. Newman called out. "You wanna come down and look at this, Dad? It's pretty cool."

Without letting go of my hand, he squatted and slid down my legs just a bit, peeking over the blanket.

"Holy shit." He breathed heavily. "It's here. I can see it."

Two more seconds of pushing and I felt the head come out, sending a tidal wave of relief over me as I struggled to catch my breath. I couldn't see Dr. Newman, but I knew exactly what she was doing as she squished and wiggled the shoulders to fit them through.

"Okay, Kacie. One more tiny push and you'll know whether you have a boy or a girl," she instructed.

This push wasn't nearly as tough as the others. I barely had to struggle and the baby slid out into Dr. Newman's arms. I waited a couple of seconds and heard the best noise ever—a screaming newborn.

"It's a girl!" Dr. Newman called out, palming the baby's chest as she wiped her down and quickly cleaned out her mouth. That pissed her off, making her scream even louder. I lay in the bed, completely exhausted but mustering up just enough strength to squeeze Brody's hand. He sat back down next to me, and it was the first time I noticed the tears streaming down his face too.

"She's so beautiful, Kacie. Just like you." He leaned down and kissed my forehead over and over. "Thank you. Thank you for taking such good care of our little girl. She's the luckiest baby on the planet and she doesn't even know it yet."

"Of course she is," I said softly. "She already has a castle in her backyard."

"Here you go, Dad." Dr. Newman handed her to Brody. "I have to clean Kacie up a bit, but I'll give you guys a minute."

My mom walked over and kissed my cheek, then the baby's cheek, then Brody's cheek again. "I'm gonna step out. I'll come back in a little bit. You guys need time, okay?"

"Thanks, Mom. I love you."

She blew me a kiss and slipped out the door.

My heart swelled as I watched Brody look at his daughter for the first time. His eyes took in every detail of her little face. He put his pinkie finger in her tiny hand and her fingertips turned white as she squeezed as hard as she could.

"She's got good reflexes." He sniffed, grinning at me. "Gonna be a hockey player."

I laughed and grimaced in pain.

"Sorry," he apologized. "You okay?"

"Just sore." I smiled.

"If you want to come over here, she's gonna get her first bath as I clean Kacie up, okay?" Taylor put her hand gently on Brody's shoulder, directing him to the warming table.

That was the last thing I remember before dozing off.

After a quick yet rejuvenating nap, the baby got a bath and it was time to nurse her. She latched on immediately and ate for a solid half hour before passing right out as they were moving us to our private room.

"This place is pretty swanky." Brody laughed as he inspected the room, opening and closing all the cabinets and checking out the pull-out bed for him.

"Knock, knock." My mom peeked her head in the door. "Can we come in?"

"Of course." Brody waved her in.

She came in, her eyes darting around the room, looking for the baby, with Lucy, Piper, and Fred right behind her. "I know it's almost dinnertime; we won't stay long. They just wanted to meet her, and of course, I wanted to hold her one more time." Mom snickered.

"Where is she?" Piper started interrogating us before she was all the way in the room.

"Right here," I answered, nodding my head toward our new daughter, asleep in my arms.

Lucy and Piper circled around me, standing on their tippy-toes to see her, as Brody videoed with his phone. Their eyes were wide, grinning at their new baby sister.

"What's her name?" Lucy asked.

I looked up at Brody and smiled. "Go ahead."

"Her name is Emma. Isn't she cute?"

"She has a tiny head." Piper craned her neck to the side, trying to get a better view of Emma's head.

"It didn't feel so tiny a few hours ago," I mumbled under my breath.

Brody chuckled at my joke. "You guys wanna hold her?"

Their heads nodded up and down like bobblehead dolls as they climbed up on the couch excitedly. Brody took Emma from my arms and gently set her in both Lucy's and Piper's arms, right in the middle. "Okay, smile." He took a step back and snapped the first picture of all of our girls together. "Three more and I can start my own hockey team." He winked at me.

"Try telling me that when I'm not high on narcotics, okay?" I joked.

"She smiled at me," Piper squealed proudly.

"It's probably just gas, baby," my mom said to her. "It's too early for her to be smiling."

"Gas?" Piper curled her nose up. "Like . . . farts?"

Everyone in the room laughed.

"Yes, like farts," my mom answered.

"Sometimes I smile when I fart too," Lucy quipped.

Brody laughed and held his hand out to Lucy for a high-five. "You and me both, kiddo."

After an hour-long visit, I'd had all I could handle and needed a nap.

"I'm sorry, Mom." I felt bad kicking everyone out, but I was so far past tired I felt like I could sleep for three days straight.

"No, don't apologize. We're gonna take the girls out to dinner and then go home and hang out. Zach said he'd take them next weekend instead, if that's okay?"

I nodded, trying to keep my eyes open. "Thanks, Mom."

"You're welcome, sweetie."

Lucy and Piper gave me careful hugs on the way out.

Fred came over and peeked down at Emma, who was passed out in my arms. "You done good, kid. She's pretty cute." He slapped a kiss on top of my head, shook Brody's hand, and was out the door.

"Here, let me take her." Brody lifted Emma out of my arms and sat down with her on his pullout bed. "Close your eyes for a bit."

"I will. I'm just enjoying the quiet right now." I blinked slowly, taking in the sight of him snuggling with our daughter.

The evening news was on the TV and Brody stared up at it, a sneaky smirk appearing on his face. His smile was contagious, and I couldn't help but grin right along with him.

"Penny for your thoughts?" I had to know.

He nodded toward the TV. "They were just talking about the weather for the weekend. I was wondering what size Emma would be."

"For what?"

He shrugged nonchalantly. "They're calling for rain. Gonna be a lot of puddles out there. She needs pink rain boots like her big sisters."

"She's got a while before she'll be ready to jump in puddles." I giggled, picturing tiny rain boots in my head. "What are you doing?"

He'd set Emma down on the couch and pulled his shirt off, exposing his cut chest. Wiggling Emma's blanket loose from her chest area, he laid her on top of him, skin to skin.

"I read that book, that *What to Expect* book, and it said it's really good for babies to be skin to skin with their parents, especially dads, since we don't nurse."

"You read that book?" I asked, surprised by the revelation. *I* hadn't even read that book.

"Hell yeah. I wanted to be prepared." He was talking to me, but taking selfies of him and Emma. "Kacie, you should lie down and rest."

"I will. One more question." I shifted myself up in my bed. "I started to ask, but then Little Murphy decided she'd had enough of my uterus. How did you get here so fast? I thought Fred wasn't able to reach you."

"We never did talk, but he left me a voice mail telling me your water broke in the kitchen. Then my phone died."

Thinking back to Fred's face as he stared at the puddle on the floor made me snicker. "He was so freaked out."

"I could tell in his message. He's usually very calm, but he was all kinds of flustered. Anyway, it was like a messed-up version of *Planes, Trains, and Automobiles*, minus the trains. I could *not* get a flight out of Chicago that would get me home before tomorrow and they had no available private planes, so I took a cab up to the Milwaukee airport and chartered a private plane from there."

A tiny lump parked itself in the middle of my throat. "You did?"

His eyes shifted from Emma to me. "Of course. And let me tell you, it was the longest five hours of my life." He swallowed hard, looking back down at Emma. "Once I charged my phone, I kept trying to call Fred and your mom and you, but I couldn't get through to anyone. I didn't know if I missed it or what, but I prayed the whole way that I hadn't."

I wasn't sure if it was the hormones or the overwhelming sense of love and gratitude I was feeling, but my eyes filled with tears. "I can't believe you did all that for her. For us."

"Watching her come into this world was the most amazing thing I've ever seen. I'm so glad I was able to get here in time."

"Me too." I sniffled.

"And I gotta be honest, I thought it was gonna be gross, but I was wrong. It was *so* cool. I can't wait to see it again."

"See it again? I'm gonna need a break for a while after that one."

The corner of his lip pulled up in an adorable smirk. "I told you I read that book. You got six weeks, tops."

ACKNOWLEDGMENTS

First and foremost, thank you *so* much to Pam Carrion and The Book Avenue for the hours you've spent organizing my cover reveal, blog tour, teasers, and everything else. I'm absolutely crazy about you, Angry Kitty *and* Bob Saget.

Melanie Codina, Michelle Finkle, and Melissa Brown: I can't thank you enough for taking the time to read this book ahead of time. All of your ideas and suggestions helped make this book what it is. Thank you from the absolute bottom of my heart.

Whitney, my mudneck Twinkie: you're such an amazing friend, and I love you, and your boner, dearly.

Michelle Finkle: Where do I begin? What started as beta reading *Room For You* turned into an amazing friendship, and I truly do not know where I would be without you. You're honest, thorough, and creative as a beta reader. More importantly you are funny, sweet, and loyal as a friend. You've talked me off the ledge more times than I can count, and for that I'll be forever grateful. I love you to pieces, Gayle.

Melissa Brown: who would've known at eight years old, when we stood on that softball field together, that twenty-five years later this is where we would be? There's no one I'd rather be surfing through this crazy amazing career with. Thank you so much for being my constant right-hand man.

Happy Driggs: Namaste, asshole.

Megan Ward: Good or bad, we did it . . . again! Thank you so much for being the absolute best editor. Your eagle eye is second to none, but your friendship means way more. Thank you for always sticking by my side and giving me a kick in the ass when I needed it. XOXO

ABOUT THE AUTHOR

Photo © 2014 Stacey Houston Photography

Bestselling author Beth Ehemann lives in the northern suburbs of Chicago with her husband and four children. A lover of martinis and all things Chicago Cubs, she can be found reading or honing her photography skills when she's not sitting in front of her computer writing—or on Pinterest. The novella *Room for Just a Little Bit More* is the final installment of her popular Cranberry Inn series, which includes the novels *Room for You* and *Room for More*.

Contact her at: authorbethehemann@yahoo.com
Or follow her on:
Facebook: www.facebook.com/bethehemann
Twitter: @bethehemann
Instagram: @bethehemann
www.bethehemann.com